The Summer Before Boys

ALSO BY NORA RALEIGH BASKIN

Anything But Typical
The Truth About My Bat Mitzvah

The Summer
Before Boys

NORA RALEIGH BASKIN

Simon & Schuster Books for Young Readers
New York London Toronto Sydney New Delhi

SIMON & SCHUSTER BOOKS FOR YOUNG READERS
An imprint of Simon & Schuster Children's Publishing Division
1230 Avenue of the Americas, New York, New York 10020
This book is a work of fiction. Any references to historical events, real people, or real locales are used fictitiously. Other names, characters, places, and incidents are products of the author's imagination, and any resemblance to actual events or locales or persons, living or dead, is entirely coincidental.
Copyright © 2011 by Nora Raleigh Baskin
All rights reserved, including the right of reproduction in whole or in part in any form.
SIMON & SCHUSTER BOOKS FOR YOUNG READERS is a trademark of Simon & Schuster, Inc.
For information about special discounts for bulk purchases, please contact Simon & Schuster Special Sales at 1-866-506-1949 or business@simonandschuster.com.
The Simon & Schuster Speakers Bureau can bring authors to your live event. For more information or to book an event, contact the Simon & Schuster Speakers Bureau at 1-866-248-3049 or visit our website at www.simonspeakers.com.
Also available in a Simon & Schuster Books for Young Readers hardcover edition
Book design by Chloë Foglia
The text for this book is set in Horley.
Manufactured in the United States of America
0312 OFF
First Simon & Schuster Books for Young Readers paperback edition April 2012
2 4 6 8 10 9 7 5 3 1
The Library of Congress has cataloged the hardcover edition as follows:
Baskin, Nora Raleigh.
The summer before boys / Nora Raleigh Baskin.
p. cm.
Audience: Ages 9–12.
Summary: Twelve-year-old best friends and relatives, Julia and Eliza are happy to spend the summer together while Julia's mother is serving in the National Guard in Iraq but when they meet a neighborhood boy, their close relationship begins to change.
ISBN 978-1-4169-8673-7 (hc)
1. Preteens—Juvenile fiction. 2. Girls—Juvenile fiction. [1. Best friends—Fiction. 2. Friendship—Fiction. 3. Families of military personnel—Fiction. 4. Interpersonal relations—Fiction. 5. Conduct of life—Fiction.] I. Title.
PZ7.B29233Su 2011
813.6—dc22
[[Fic]]
2010045688
ISBN 978-1-4169-8674-4 (pbk)
ISBN 978-1-4424-2383-1 (eBook)

*To the women
of the United States Armed Forces,
and to their children*

Acknowledgments

There are many people I would like to thank deeply:

Alexandra Cooper, my editor extraordinaire.

Nancy Gallt, my wonderful agent.

And, of course: Will the real Julia (Sandler) and Eliza (Sandler) please stand up? I not only stole their names but some of their childhood imagination, and it belongs to them.

Lee Blake, for giving me free access to the hotel for a day, a wonderful lunch, and all that time on the phone discussing the details.

Janet Yusko, for reminding me about our very own make-believe world of Lester and Lynette (where did we ever get those names?)

Cindy Rider, who allowed me the most magical summer at Mohonk Mountain House *before boys* and a friendship I will never forget.

Charity Tahmaseb, fellow author and friend, for answering my nonstop questions about the military and about women serving in particular.

Fran Arrowsmith, nurse practitioner, civilian and military, and long-time friend.

Once again, to Tony Abbott and Elise Broach, who listen so patiently (while we eat long breakfasts at the Bluebird) and offer the best writing (and life) advice a friend could ever ask for.

And for anyone wishing more information or to help women veterans please contact:

http://www.homesforthebrave.org.

"War is not healthy for children and other living things."

—*Lorraine Schneider, 1966*

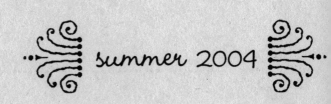

summer 2004

My Aunt Louisa, who is really my sister, snored like a machine with a broken part, a broken part that kept cycling around in a shuddering, sputtering rhythm.

"Whistle with me," Eliza said into the dark.

"What?"

We lay together in bed, in Eliza's room that was really not a room, but a part of the den that had been sectioned off with a thin portable wall. Each night either Aunt Louisa, or Uncle Bruce, who is really my brother-in-law, pulled out "the wall," like stretching an accordion as far as it would go. Then Eliza would yank her bed right out of the couch and we would both slip under the cool sheets and the thin cotton blanket.

It was summer.

The summer I spent living with Eliza, who is really my niece, but since we are both twelve years old that feels kind of stupid. So we just tell everyone we are cousins.

And it was the summer before boys.

"If you whistle, she stops snoring," Eliza told me.

"Really?"

"Really. Watch."

Mostly Eliza was my best friend. We both went to New Hope Middle School, but I lived in town, on Main Street. And Eliza lived way up here, right at the base of the Cayuga Mountain, right at the gatehouse entrance to the Mohawk Mountain Lodge. She lived at the foot of a magical place and now I got to live there too. For the whole summer.

Because my dad, who is technically Eliza's grandfather, had to work.

And so there was no one home to watch me.

And because my mom got deployed to Iraq nine and a half months ago.

Eliza whistled one long, clear, unwavering note. It floated out of the perfect circle she made with her lips and into the air. Her whistle slipped right under "the wall" that didn't quite touch the floor, or the ceiling, so that Eliza's room was lit with flickering gray light from the television set left on all night. Her whistle carried through the den and into Aunt Louisa and Uncle Bruce's bedroom.

And the snoring stopped, just like that.

"It worked!" I said.

"Every time."

"Does it last?"

"For a little while."

I poked my feet out of the bottom of our sheet and thin white cotton blanket, careful not to pull the covers from Eliza.

"I'm hot," I said.

Eliza was already standing beside the bed, her bare feet on the wood floor. "Then let's go outside," she whispered to me.

Her white nightgown wrinkled and clung to her thighs—it was so sticky out—her scabby summer knees were showing. Her hair was sleepy, pulled from its ponytail so it poufed up around the back of her head and glowed like a halo in the unnatural light from the TV.

"What time is it?"

"Don't you know? It's time to go outside," Eliza said. "Run!"

And we ran. I ran. Past the TV, past the bedroom door, into the kitchen and right onto the big crack in linoleum that pinched my big toe.

"Ouch," I said.

"You've got to jump over that," Eliza reminded me. "C'mon—"

We ran until we were flying.

Light elves, higher with each leap—onto the wet grass, into the hot summer night. We were the fairies that lived in the woods beyond the yard, hidden under the fallen trees, making homes of the leaves and twigs. Growing wings of glistening, glowing gossamer, as we felt ourselves lifted from the ground.

"Look at me," Eliza said. She lifted her arms and twirled around. She threw back her head. The bottom of her nightgown unstuck from her legs and spun out around her.

"Look at me," I said. And when I looked up I saw the sky, dotted with sparkling stars and a sliver of the moon that looked like someone had tried to erase it but couldn't quite get it all. I arched my neck and turned around and around in place.

We spun until we couldn't stand up and we both fell together, down the hill where Uncle Bruce parked his truck, and we lay there at the edge of the lawn to catch our breath. I was wearing a white nightgown identical to Eliza's—worn and pilled. I picked off pieces of grass, one by one—looking so closely—and I could barely make out the faded kittens and puppies in the fabric. Little pink kittens and little blue puppies, when this nightgown must have been brand-new.

I wondered if Aunt Louisa had bought it, if she had bought two, thinking of me, one day, spending nights at her house. Had she ever thought her father would have another little girl, twenty-two years after she was born, with another wife who became another mother? Or maybe it was just another hand-me-down from a whole other mother to another little girl altogether that Aunt Louisa picked up from Goodwill when she found out I would be staying here for the summer.

"Tomorrow we can go up to the hotel," Eliza said. "It's check-in day. There'll be a lot of people driving up. But Roger will pick us up for sure, if he sees us walking."

"Who?"

"The van driver."

"Oh, right." I liked to pretend I belonged there too.

The mosquitoes began to smell our sweat, found our skin, and feasted. I scratched at my ankles and my left elbow and my forehead, but I didn't want to go in. I wanted to keep looking at the moon, to memorize it and fill in the empty space.

What time is it?

Of course, I knew what time it was.

I always knew what time it was.

In Baghdad.

Or Ramadi. Or Tikrit. Or Fallujah. But my mother can't tell me where she is. She calls and sends me e-mails, but she isn't allowed to tell me where she is.

It's morning time in Iraq right now.

I know what time it is.

My mother was probably getting up and making her bunk. And maybe eating breakfast already. She tells me she hates the powdered eggs, but they are okay with lots of ketchup.

She can't see the moon at all anymore. The sun is shining now where she is and I think that right at this very second she might be thinking of me. And I wonder if she is as worried about her forgetting my face as I am about forgetting hers.

two

The walk to the Mountain Lodge was just over a mile from Eliza's house, and if we had been ready to go at five thirty in the morning we could always get a ride with Uncle Bruce. But we never got up that early. Summer is for sleeping late and not having to get up, and not having anywhere you have to be.

And now it was already hot like yesterday, and the day before that.

Three cars had already passed us by—not one was the hotel van—but we didn't mind.

"Imagine in the old days," Eliza began, "when ladies and men rode up this road in buggies. Horse and carriages."

I loved to imagine that. If I were one of those ladies, or a daughter of one of those ladies, I'd be wearing a long dress, and high button boots. I'd have a hat for sure. And a parasol. There were old photographs all over the hotel, of the hotel and of the Smith family who had built and owned the hotel—and still did—and of people, women and children and men, swimming or riding horses, or just standing very, very still while somebody with a big huge camera hid under a black piece of fabric and said, "Now don't move."

And I'd still be twelve years old but in those days I'd already be a young woman. I'd have put away my paper dolls and jacks. I'd already be learning to sew and serve tea and do only ladylike things.

"Can we sneak into tea today?" I asked Eliza.

"Definitely."

Eliza's dad, Uncle Bruce, worked at Mohawk. He was the man who made sure the three hundred and thirteen wooden gazebos (they called them summer houses) that appeared all over the grounds, all along the trail up to the tower, all around the gardens, and even here and there along this road, were maintained. Every intricate lattice of gnarled wood had to be perfect. Every floorboard safe, every shingle of every thatched roof nailed into place. And Eliza's dad did that, five days a week. It took him the whole week to get to all of them. The following week he did the same thing all over again. And there is always something to repair, he said. Most everything at Mohawk was old. The Mountain Lodge was built in 1862 and it pretty much looked exactly as it had then. There were no candy machines, no big screen TVs, no chrome, no plastic. If Louisa May Alcott or Laura Ingalls Wilder stepped into this hotel there would be nothing to surprise them. They would feel right at home. They wouldn't even know any time had gone by at all.

Eliza had grown up at Mohawk Mountain Lodge, so she knew everyone who worked there and nobody stopped her from going anywhere. Walking up the road to the hotel I thought, *This is going to be a safe day.*

A good day.

Sweat dripped down the back of my shirt but it didn't bother me that much. I wore the same cut-off jean shorts that had been too big on me last year and new but already dirty sneakers. I couldn't even remember what T-shirt I had thrown on this morning. What I really looked like didn't matter, because walking on that road it could be any year, any century we wanted to imagine.

Eliza and I.

And we had the whole summer ahead of us.

The dirt road was dusty and the heat seemed to shimmy from the rocks and distort the air. The lazy overhanging bushes and tree branches didn't bother to shade us. They looked too hot, too tired to even try.

This part of the road was for two-way traffic, but when we got to the bend, where the abandoned cement quarry was still visible, the road would split. It would be one-way the rest of the way up and by then we would know we were almost there, quarter mile to go.

"Almost there," Eliza announced.

But the sky was getting very dark.

"It's gonna rain." And just as I said that a huge, single drop of water thumped onto the dry dirt road. Another right on my nose, and almost immediately a loud clap of thunder sounded from above.

By the time we reached the hairpin turn we were both soaked, my T-shirt like another layer of skin. Even my socks squished inside my sneakers. Without a word to each other we broke into a gallop.

"My underwear is wet now!" Eliza shouted. She was ahead of me.

"Mine too." I laughed.

"Eliza, does your mother know you're out here in this?" I heard the voice first. A forest green van had pulled up beside us and the driver was leaning out the window.

We were still running, the van moving slowly along beside us. It was filled with guests on their way to the Mountain Lodge for the week. With the sound of the rain, I hadn't heard the engine coming up from behind, but now the windshield wipers swept back and forth, squeaking rubber. I saw the faces peering out the window at us, an old couple, a young mother with her little boy on her lap. Two boys, close to my age, maybe a little older, looking as bored as they could manage. I quickly looked away.

"Yeah," Eliza shouted back. "But it wasn't raining when we left."

I guessed this was Roger, the driver.

"Well, you two get in." He pulled the van ahead of us and over to the side of the road. He let us squat down by the van door since we were too wet to take a real seat. Besides, they were all taken by guests.

Roger said, "Stay still, you two. Stay sitting."

The van was air-conditioned and the goose bumps rose on my legs and arms so fast I could feel them pinch my skin. The two boys were looking at us. One had blond hair and the other was dark-haired. I shifted and tried to face the door. I suddenly remembered what T-shirt I had put on this morning and I regretted it. It had a picture of the Little Mermaid on the front and it felt suddenly too small. It was wet against my chest. I was glad I was wearing an undershirt underneath, the one I had slept in.

Where were the ladies in horse-drawn carriages and their men holding the parasols above their heads? My skin suddenly stuck out all over my body, my legs, my arms, my back, my neck.

I pressed my legs closer together and hugged my arms around them. Where are my white petticoats, my ivory-colored dress, and lace shawl that would have covered my whole body? Only my ankles might have shown, and my ankles looked okay, didn't they?

Don't all ankles look the same? Wasn't there a time when just an exposed ankle would have been scandalous?

Where was my broad-rimmed hat with the wide blue ribbon that would have hidden my face when I tipped my chin down?

"Hey, Roger, can you go a little faster?" Eliza said. "I'm getting pins and needles in my feet and my bottom is killing me."

"Sit tight there, girl. We're here."

The van braked with a lurch, at the entrance to Mohawk Mountain Lodge, just as the rain stopped and the sun broke through the mist and clouds and the last droplets of rain. Somebody once wrote, the secret to life is good timing.

I think they are right.

Because bad timing stinks.

three

My mom joined the National Guard on August 14, 2001. It was right after my dad got laid off from IBM and just before he found another job as the manager of Lloyd's Gas and Service station. I was nine years old.

Bad timing.

"I'll only be gone one weekend a month," my mom told me. "And two weeks in summer. Like going to summer camp." She was kneeling down in front of me, zipping up my jacket. I had trouble with zippers then. I couldn't get the metal thing inside the other metal thing, at least not so it could work.

I had tears in my eyes as if I had known—but how could I have known?—that there would be a war. Because back then I just didn't want my mother to go away. Not for one weekend. Not for one hour. Not ever.

"It's extra money," she told me. "So I can buy you the things you need and maybe some things you just want. Like that Powerpuff Girls lunch box?"

And that made me happy. How sick is that? I was suddenly all excited about getting a Powerpuff lunch box because I really wanted one for my first day of third grade.

I knew something had changed, but I got my lunch box—and for a while it was still okay.

Once a month my mom went to Freehold, New Jersey, for training. Lots of troops were going to Afghanistan after 9/11, but real soldiers, active duty, reservists, not National Guard. Not weekend soldiers. Not my mom.

Plus, Dad and I got to eat at Friendly's for dinner those Friday and Saturday nights. I actually looked forward to it. My meal came with a free ice-cream sundae, hard candy eyes, upside-down cone for a hat.

And for the next couple of summers, my mom went to "summer camp" and I went to stay with Uncle Bruce and Aunt Louisa (and of course Eliza, who, for the longest time, I thought was my cousin) because my dad worked all day and they couldn't leave me alone every day for two whole weeks.

Those were the best two weeks. Back then we were too young to hang around up at the hotel by ourselves, so every morning Aunt Louisa (who, I think, was even a little fatter back then, before she went on Weight Watchers) got up and drove us down the mountain and into town, to the Elting Memorial Library.

Eliza and I ran inside and straight to the back, to the children's section. It was cool and musty back there. It was in the old stone house section of the library. You could see the stones from the inside, bumpy and coated white with thick shiny paint.

Aunt Louisa waited in the car with the air conditioning blowing on her full force, while Eliza and I grabbed *Little House on the Prairie*, or *Anne of Green Gables*, or *Little Women*.

And every summer my mom and I, both, would come home with stories.

But three years later, the day she left for Iraq, everything changed. I knew it when she cried and cried the night before. When my dad cried too. When we all drove to that big gym in Newburgh and stood with all those hundreds of other crying grown-ups.

My mom hugged us so tight I could hardly breathe and I didn't want to. I didn't want to be the one to let go first. So I kept my face buried in between my mom and my dad and I said to myself, over and over: *Everything will be all right if she doesn't put on her hat. If she just doesn't put on her hat.*

I hated her hat. It was tucked into the back pocket of her fatigues, as if she knew.

Just don't put on that ugly hat.

I wasn't crazy about the whole uniform, the mixing of tan and green and gray that covered her body from her neck to her feet and was supposed to help her blend in. To hide. To protect her.

To protect her?

So as long as she didn't put that little patrol cap on her head, I could still see her hair. And if I could still separate her face from the uniform—then everything would be okay.

"I gotta go now," my mom said.

I couldn't look at her face. I could hear the sadness choking her voice. I kept my head down.

My dad whispered something to my mom and then my mom told us both, "I'm going to go now. You two turn and head out. I'm going to go now. Everything is going to be all right. Don't turn back around."

And I didn't. So I don't know if she put that cap on her head or not. It was the last time I saw her. That was seven months ago. *She will be home by the end of August, before summer is over,* they promised.

She'd be home in twelve months, by the end of that August.

She promised.

four

Everyone got out of the van at the beginning of the long entrance to the hotel, by one of many gardens—the one with mini-labyrinth of tall evergreen hedges and the hundreds of baby rose bushes. Because Eliza and I were on the steps, we were the first to stand up and get out. Directly in front of us white steam from the rain hovered just above the wet grass. Overhead, the sun was filtering down through the clouds in long fingers of light and the heat was already rising again as if it had never been gone at all, only hiding. Waiting.

And then there was the hotel.

It loomed too high and too far on each end to take it in completely from so close. There was the wooden section and the hundreds of green shuttered windows, which were the guests' rooms, but all you could really see, standing right here by the entrance, was the stone archway and the stone porch. Stones that looked too big to be called stones—more like boulders—yet someone had once, a long time ago, placed them here and built this hotel around it. Under the massive stone arch, a damp coolness welcomed the carriages whose delicate spoked wheels rolled to a stop.

In those days guests would have ridden all day, first on the train from the city into town and then up the bumpy roads right to this very spot. They would be dusty and tired. Or just excited and jumpy, anxious to stretch their legs.

"Julia, c'mon." Eliza called to me. She was already up on the porch. Technically, we really weren't supposed to be in the hotel itself, we weren't paying guests, so the quicker and smoother we slipped inside the better. I knew this. So why did I feel like I wanted to turn around and look back at those two boys? They were just stepping down, so I figured they waited until everyone else had gotten off and, even then, they were proceeding very slowly. The blond one pushed the darker-haired boy as he got to the last step, just enough to make him stumble. They were brothers for sure, I thought. I hurried to catch up with Eliza, through the wide glass doors.

It was cool inside, dark and cool, thick with the smell of old wood and old wool. I could see hundreds of old-fashioned shoes walking over this very carpet, over thousands of days and millions of hours. But right now the hall was nearly empty. There was a couple standing at the registration desk checking in. The man, in a blue jacket, was talking to someone behind the counter and the woman, who was wearing all black—cropped pants and a tight tank top—was standing, with her feet straddling her luggage as if someone might just run by and grab it. They must be from New York City.

Our own footsteps thumped past and echoed down the hall. We were headed to the gift shop.

"Girls, girls. Where's the fire? What's the rush?" It was Pam, the ice-cream lady. Pam worked in the gift shop. She sat all day on her stool and rang up the people who were buying postcards and rock candy on a stick. Or Mohawk sweatshirts or stuffed animals that said I ♥ MOHAWK. Or a magnifying glass or a boxed set of little rocks. But we called her the ice-cream lady because she gave us free ice cream.

There was a big freezer that slid open on top and inside were boxes and boxes of different kinds of ice cream. Fudgsicles, which aren't really ice cream. Drumsticks. Push-Up Pops, not ice cream either. Ice-cream sandwiches. Chipwiches. Klondike Bars. Good Humor Chocolate Eclairs. And then there were lots of those stupid-baby ice creams in the shape of some cartoon character that got real messy and dripped red and purple all over your arm before you could ever get to the bubble-gum nose.

"Hi, Pam," I said without looking up. My eyes just fell over all the objects in the gift shop. It was impossible not to look. There was just so much of everything. Pens and stationery. Stuffed animals. Cups and saucers. Aprons. Jewelry. Soaps, lots of pretty soaps. In here, it smelled like flowers and lemons and cinnamon.

"Julia, you're here for the whole summer this year, aren't you?"

"She is," Eliza answered. "Her mom is still in Iraq and her dad is working. So she is staying with us all summer."

I knew what was going to follow.

"Iraq, my goodness," Pam said. "You must be so proud."

I wasn't proud. I wasn't proud at all. I mean I was. I was proud. I was proud that my mom was in the army, that she was fighting for our country. That she was so brave. And had given up so much to help other people, to protect our country. But no one really understood. They thought they did. Proud sounds like a happy thing and I wasn't happy that my mother was in Iraq.

But I was proud, too, so I said so.

"Yeah, I guess." And I must have looked like I was about to cry because I felt Eliza put her arm around me. Her shirt was still damp from the rain. She smelled like a body that had been sleeping, and a body that got wet, and that ran and that played. It was familiar and I was glad she was with me.

"I'm sorry," Eliza said. I knew she meant she was sorry for bringing it up, and sorry that it made me feel sad, but she was also sorry for me.

She was sorry my mom was so far away. Sorry there was a war and some people didn't come back, or they came back without their leg, or their hand, or their eyes. Or their memories. There was this lady, Mrs. Jaffe, who came to our school once a month just to meet with kids who had a mom or a dad on active duty, but me and Peter Vos were the only two kids in the whole school. Even though it felt good to talk to someone who knew what I was going through, I just wanted to get back to my class.

Eliza was the only one who really seemed to understand. She was sorry just for me and to tell the truth having someone feel sorry for me wasn't so bad.

"I'm okay," I said. I didn't want to feel the stinging behind my eyes.

"How about a little ice cream," Pam broke in. "On me." Which was funny since it was always "on her" but we had all agreed some time ago, without ever saying so, to act like it was the first time. The only time.

Until next time.

Eliza picked the Snoopy on a stick with the black collar and bubble-gum nose. And I did too.

five

Eliza and I ate our ice creams on the porch. The rockers were for the old people and paying customers, so we sat on the porch steps overlooking the lake. When the lake was still, and the sun was shining, like it was now, the water was a mirror and the whole hotel hung upside down in the perfect glass for all time.

"Whatcha want to do?" Eliza asked me.

"Nothing. How about you?"

"Nothing, either."

So that's what we did.

For the longest while we just sat there, our ice creams finished and only invisible but sticky remnants on our fingers and chins. Guests and staff walked by, up and down the stone steps, and all around us. The staff all wore green polo shirts with the neatly stitched Mohawk Mountain Lodge insignia on the left and a rectangular name tag pinned on the right.

Everybody else was guests, except for me and Eliza.

And Mrs. Smith.

"Girls. The stairs?" Mrs. Smith didn't have to use very many words. She was tiny, but packed into a compact body that commanded attention and fear. She was probably old, too, but it was hard to tell. Her hair was cut short and tight, and was jet-black, but then again so was my grandmother's. You didn't want to stare at Mrs. Smith's face long enough to really figure it out.

She was a Smith, of course, of the Smith Family who had built this hotel two hundred years ago. Anything and everything having to do with the Mohawk Mountain Lodge went through her first, and last. I suppose we were clogging up the stairs. When Mrs. Smith shook her head, we just took off.

"Wanna go on one of the trails?" Eliza asked me. We slowed from our run and were walking that way anyway, heading in the direction of the hiking trails and the walking paths, leaving the hotel, the stairs, and Pam the ice cream lady farther behind us.

"Sure."

We liked to take the tended walking path, the tiny road cut into the woods, scattered carefully with the tiny, sharp pieces of shale from the quarry below. It twisted in and out, but always up and up until you reached the very top. Even the old ladies and men could manage the walking paths, slowly, but they walked along and made their way to the tower where you could look out onto four states. I don't know which ones but they say it's four.

But real hikers, even professional mountain climbers, came into town and up to Mohawk to hike the real trails, The Falls, The Lemon Squeeze, The Cat Walk, and Death Valley.

"It's so hot again," I said.

"Yeah, but imagine if we had to wear those long dresses like in the olden days."

"And petticoats," I added, keeping my eyes ahead and focused down. "And wool stockings, even in the summer." Somehow this made my world more bearable.

The path grew narrower then wider and then narrower again. In very steep sections, there were railroad ties holding the shale in place and creating steps for a giant. And every so often the path jutted gently toward lakeside and presented the walker with a wooden gazebo to stop and rest.

Eliza and I rested in every single one.

"Nothing is different in the world," Eliza said. She hung her arms over the twisted branch of tree that served as the railing.

I thought to myself, *No, everything is different.*

Our country was at war. It was far away from here, and most people never even thought about it, but it never rested. And every day, soldiers and doctors and military police and cooks and engineers came home different from when they left. Mrs. Jaffe who came to my school tried to get me and Peter to talk about it but neither one of us wanted to.

"My dad's a hero," Peter said. "He's really brave and there's nothing I want to talk about."

"He certainly is, Peter. No one is ever going to say differently. I just thought you might want to talk a little bit about how you feel these days, alone in the house with your mom and sister. It must be hard sometimes."

Peter shot the lady a look—but it didn't seem to stop her. It was like she was expecting that.

"You don't live on a military base. Neither of you." Mrs. Jaffe looked at me. "You don't have the support system. Most of these kids don't even know there's a war going on."

I was relieved when the bell rang. And so was Peter. He wiped his eyes and darted out the door.

Nothing is different in the world, Eliza had said.

But even though Eliza was wrong and Mrs. Jaffe was right, I let Eliza's white and faded jean shorts turn to muslin. I watched her messy, long hair collect under a make-believe wide-brimmed hat. If we had a parasol, I saw that, too. If I could feel the laced-up knickers under my dress, then maybe nothing in the world would be different.

"Father says exercise is good for the mind," Eliza said, "and body. Healthful living."

"A wise man, indeed," I said, because in the old days people said things like that, like "indeed." We stepped out of the gazebo and continued upward. The sun was now well above the trees, clinging to one spot, it felt, burning right above our heads.

"Mother will reprimand us if our dresses are so dirty," Eliza said.

I looked down at the eyelet hem of my white skirt, splattered with damp mud and specks of shale, my flat ballet slippers nearly filthy.

"Oh, who cares?" I shouted. "We are free!"

"We are free. No tutoring for a month. No sewing lessons all summer. No dance lessons. We can swim today if we want."

"Or take out a rowboat."

"Or sneak into the kitchen."

We were nearly at the top, the highest point of all Mohawk Mountain, where you could see those four states. The very top, where the stone watchtower reached straight up into the sky, where you could climb the winding stairs, and then walk out on the stone terrace, lean your body out into the world and fly.

That summer before boys, I knew I could fly if I had to. I knew my legs would work, my arms would move, my chest would fill with air. My skin could bear the bites of a million mosquitoes, splinters, and sunburns. My body never let me down.

"Julia, there's something I have to tell you. I've wanted to tell you."

We were out of breath from taking the stairs two at a time.

"Mother says it's time for me to devote myself to my studies and housework." Eliza placed her hands on the cold stone wall, but didn't stretch any farther. "She's says it's time for me to become a young lady."

"What does that mean?" I asked. A million real and make-believe thoughts jumped into my head. It was impossible to tell them apart. No more games? No more hikes? No more running outside in our nightclothes and holding fireflies in our cupped hands?

"I think she wants me to start entertaining suitors." Eliza hung her head.

"No," I said in disbelief.

"It isn't up to me, Julia. You know that. If you had a mother it would be the same for you. We are nearly thirteen years old. You are free. I am not."

"Then we shall make a pact," I said. I pulled Eliza away from the wall. I took her two hands in mine and brought them to my chest. "We will be friends forever. Never will any boy come between us. You will turn down every suitor until your mother and father give up."

"Oh, Julia—do you think that could work? Do you?"

I loved the smile I saw come back into her eyes.

"It has to," I said.

"Then it will."

six

When we got back, it was nearly dark—but Aunt Louisa wasn't mad at us. She told me my mother had called, just two seconds earlier. I wish it had been an hour ago, or even twenty minutes. But two seconds? How can you miss something so important by two seconds?

My mother can call pretty much anytime she wants. She is a nurse and so she got to go right into the service as an officer, and now she's a first lieutenant so she gets to use the phone and computer whenever she wants. But because of the time difference she only calls once a day, if that. She must have been up very early. It must have been dark in Iraq, too—just an entirely different dark.

"She said she thought you'd be expecting her call at five," Aunt Louisa told me.

And then I remembered. I remembered that I forgot, and I realized this was the first time I had ever forgotten. Sometimes I would wait for her call that didn't come, she would tell me later what had happened. Incoming wounded, power surges or outages. Sandstorms that affected reception. Dead zones or red alerts. But I had never forgotten to wait.

And that was so much worse than missing her call.

"It's okay, sweetie," Aunt Louisa said. "Everything's fine. She just wanted to say hello and see how you were. I told her you were still up at the hotel, you'd be back soon. I told her how tan you were getting."

"It's okay, Julia," Eliza said. "She'll probably call tomorrow."

"I'm fine," I told them both. I saw them looking at each other. "I think I'll get washed up now."

When I looked in the mirror above the bathroom sink, I was surprised by how dirty my face was. There was a new tiny, red cut on my forehead and a nice smudge of dirt across my cheek, up near my eye. I wondered how long it had been there. It could have been from the lake, a piece of leaf or mud that dried there. Or from hiding in the bushes near the parking attendants' booth, where Eliza and I waited to see if those two boys from the van would come out of the hotel.

They did, but by then we had lost interest in them completely. I don't think Eliza was interested in spying on them in the first place, but she did it for me. The boys headed down to the tennis courts but neither Eliza nor I felt like following them. A few moments later the parents came out.

They were tall and short. The mom was tall and the dad was short. They were dark and light, sullen and fuming. He was sullen. She was fuming. You can always tell when grown-ups have been fighting with each other.

Right before my mother left for active duty in Iraq we all started fighting with each other. Me with my mom, my mom with my dad. My dad with me. It started about a month before, actually. It got gradually worse and worse until three days before, and then it got really bad.

My mom picked Oliver up from my floor and threw him across the room. He landed with a soft plunk by my bed. She hadn't even knocked on my door before she came in.

"Now look what you did," I screamed. I mean I really screamed. Oliver was my stuffed unidentifiable creature. I had had him since I was two. He had only one eye, assuming those had been eyes, and almost all the felt of his face was worn away. His legs and arms dangled from a big square body. He slept with me every night. "You broke him!"

"Well, maybe then you should clean your room like I've asked you to do for six days now." My mother never yells. She was yelling.

So many things crossed my mind, and of all the stupid things to say, the worst one just flew out of my mouth. "Why should I?" I shouted back.

I was so angry. My room? She was upset with me about cleaning my room, or not cleaning my room. And it wasn't that messy or anything. We had both seen it much worse and never fought about it before. Nothing made sense. The war certainly didn't make sense. What did they need my mother for? Why did there have to be a war at all? Weren't there other nurses in the world, nurses who had joined the real army?

Nurses who didn't have children at home who needed their mothers. Children like me.

So who cares about a couple pairs of jeans on the floor, a few socks, and my math workbook. And yesterday's lunch bag—it was pretty much empty.

"So why should I?" I think I even said it twice.

If I'd ever seen autumn turn to winter in a split second, or tall buildings that once stood crumble before my eyes, that's how my mother's face looked. She went from up to down, rage to sorrow, dark to empty. My dad had come in at that point to see what all the yelling was about. He stood in the doorway right behind my mom. He put his hands on her shoulders and we were like dominos in a row about to fall.

"Because," she said in a voice that wasn't hers, "I'm not always going to be here to do it for you."

That was our worst night but at least it was over. We stopped fighting then, and every day after that until we said good-bye in the gym in Newburgh.

seven

Uncle Bruce said a heat wave is defined as more than four consecutive days of weather ninety degrees or higher. We were at day six. The air conditioners in the house had not been turned off and Aunt Louisa was worried about the electric bill but she worried more about the horrible hot weather. Even inside the house, the air blasting, her skin glistened.

"Hot enough for you girls?" she said several times a day, every time she changed into another sleeveless shirt even though we weren't going anywhere.

Eliza and I hadn't walked up to the hotel since last week. We mostly stayed in the house, watching soap operas with Aunt Louisa or reading. I was nearly finished with *Eight Cousins*.

"I'm bored," Eliza announced. She put down her book, face-down, spread open—the spine ached. The blinds were pulled and the lights were off because of the heat, so it was too dark to read inside anyway. The only light came and went as the characters on *Days of Our Lives* moved from the bright hospital to the dark jailhouse.

Aunt Louisa turned from the television set. "There is no such thing as boredom."

"Oh, yeah?" Eliza said. "Well, I'm bored."

We had already made cookies three times in as many days, but the no-baking kind since Aunt Louisa didn't want us to turn on the oven. We organized Eliza's closet. We filled up the bathtub and dropped in various objects to see which would float and which would sink. We played with our village of dolls, D'Ville, and had three doll contests.

I wanted to say, "Me too. I'm bored too." But it sounded rude and ungrateful and I wasn't really Aunt Louisa's daughter or her niece. I was her sister and sometimes that just felt plain weird.

"There's too much life to be lived to be bored," Aunt Louisa told us but she had her eyes back on the twenty-four-hour soap opera channel.

Eliza rolled her eyes. "There's too much time," she moaned. "And there's nothing to do." It was all of eight fifteen in the morning.

The woman on the show had just told her fiancé that she had a son she had given up for adoption twenty years ago who had just come back into her life. So she couldn't possibly get married now, she told him, weeping.

"If we were Indian captives we'd have to walk in the heat," I told Eliza. "They would have scalped our whole family and forced us to march for days without food back to their camp."

Eliza just shrugged.

I looked over at Aunt Louisa who was just trying to watch her shows and I felt like I should do something. I wanted to seem more useful.

"We'd only find out what happened to our mother and father when we saw our mother's bright red hair lying by the side of the road," I tried.

That got her.

"That's gross. That's disgusting. That's horrible. You read too many books."

"But we were used to walking a lot and hard work from growing up in the new settlement." I kept it up. It was working. "Our dad is away on a hunting expedition. We haven't had fresh meat or milk or cheese in weeks."

"Or eggs."

"Or coffee."

"Our mom is sick," Eliza started. "She caught the summer fever. The grippe."

Neither one of us really knew what the grippe was, but we

had heard it somewhere and we knew it was really bad, like an old-fashioned sickness that they didn't have medicine for in those days.

"So we've had to carry water and boil the last of our potatoes to eat."

"We are down to only two meals a day."

I said, "Potatoes and potatoes."

The scalping was forgotten, as was the long, hard walk back to the Indian camp. Now we were on a journey to find medicine for our mother. It was her only chance. It was our only chance. We had to make the trek in one day, all the way to Doc Miller's and back before the precious liquid could get too warm and lose its power. Before our mother's fever overtook her mind like it had her wasting body.

"That's the magic," Doc Miller told us as he pressed the small brown bottle into my hands and wrapped my fingers around it. "Don't lose it. It's the only batch I have left."

"The magic," we both repeated. We knew what we had to do.

Eliza and I headed out into the brutal heat. Alas, we had no choice.

eight

We decided to go directly into the lake.

We would walk up to the hotel with our bathing suits under our shorts and beeline right down to the beach. That was our plan. We were dripping hot and bugs were swarming to our sweat by the time we reached the entrance to the hotel.

My shirt was sticking to my back right through my bathing suit and my hair was in clumps sticking to the back of my neck. We still had to walk past the spa and the platform tennis courts and the stables to get to the steep steps carved right into the cliff that led down to the beach.

I walked holding my ponytail up for a while till my arms got tired. When my neck got too hot, I held my hair up again. Eliza told me the backs of her knees were sweating. Nothing, she said, was going to keep us out of that water when we finally got there.

Except the cold, it turned out. The cold kept us from diving right into the lake and swimming out to the dock.

"It's freezing." I put the top part of my big toe into the water. Suddenly I wasn't so hot anymore.

"It's so cold."

We both stood, facing the lake, facing the rise of the cliffs on the other side, facing the spot where the sun was burning another hole in the sky. Waves of heat already shimmering in the air. It was still early. Only a few guests were here at the beach, and a couple of early swimmers, the ones that did laps across the width of the lake and back.

"Chickens." A voice seemed to come from under the stone steps.

When I turned around no one was there.

"What was that?" I asked Eliza.

"Oh, that's Michael. It's just Michael and his brother," Eliza told me.

"Who?"

"You don't know them. They go to a different school. Their dad works here too, taking care of the horses. They're really annoying. Don't even look at them."

But I did. I mean, I attempted to look.

"No one's there," I said.

"There's, like, a little opening, a little cave under the stairs. They're probably in there." Eliza took another baby step into the water. "It's freezing."

"Of course it's cold. It's a glacier lake." Michael popped out from the rocks and onto the sand. He was alone. No brother in sight.

"I know what it is, Michael." Eliza answered but she didn't take her gaze from the water. "I've been here as long as you have."

Michael had dark hair, cut so short he looked like he was in the army. He had blue eyes. I could see that from here.

"That makes you an even bigger chicken, then," he said.

"Oh, yeah? Why's that?"

"Because you're acting like you're so surprised. It was a big huge iceberg that broke off and got left behind from the Ice Age. What'd you think? An iceberg's gonna be warm? I swim every day, not like you."

I just listened. I shifted my head back and forth from Eliza to Michael, who were talking to each other as if I wasn't even there.

"That was hundreds of years ago," Eliza said.

"Millions," Michael corrected her, but I saw him looking at me. "Who's this? You guys related to each other or friends?"

Usually we don't answer that question. Over the years Eliza and I have learned when to give out the truth and when not to.

If you don't want to explain anything, if you don't want to make more conversation, then the less information the better.

"We're not friends," I just blurted out. "I'm her aunt."

Now Eliza spun around.

"Her what?" Michael asked. He came even closer.

"Nothing," Eliza answered. She narrowed her eyes and gave me a look. "Just leave us alone. We're going to go for a swim."

"No, you're not. You're both too chicken. The water's too cold for you." Michael spoke in a high-pitched whine, a girl-imitation.

He was not being very nice to us. There was nothing even all that interesting about him, except his blue eyes. But he seemed interested in us. So why then did I do what I did next?

"Maybe it's too cold for you," I said. I dipped my hand into the shallow lake and scooped it up and flung it backward. I think if Michael had not been rubbing his eyes in his make-believe "girl" cry he might have seen what I was doing and ducked out of the way. But as it was, I got him right in the face with a hand-ful of water.

"Hey," he shouted and he lunged at me, which I suppose I knew was going to happen. There was only one way out and that was in. I grabbed Eliza's hand and started heading into the freezing-cold lake, because that's what you do when you are being chased—you run.

Because this, apparently, this fluttering-in-the-stomach-I-have-no-idea-why-I-just-said-that kind of thing, is a whole different kind of magic than Doc Miller, pioneers, and Indian captives—but it felt like magic all the same.

efore my mother ever went to "summer camp"—
when September 11th was just the day after the
10th, a day before the 12th—and way before my mother left
for Iraq—we would go away in August for a week to the college
retreat in Ashokan. The three of us.

Since my mom worked at the University Health Center we
got to use a cabin, take out the boats, and borrow any camping
equipment we wanted. It's a perk, my mom said, and for the
longest time I thought a "perk" was another word for a family
vacation.

The cabin was always dark and thick-smelling when we first
stepped inside. It took a while for your eyes to adjust, but your
nose really never did. It kind of always smelled wet, like the
inside of tree would smell if I were an elf or a gnome. The start of

one particular week, I was probably five or six years old. My dad was still unloading our stuff from the car but my mom and I were so hot we just couldn't wait. Or, I didn't want to wait.

"But Daddy hasn't gotten my duffel bag," I complained. "I don't have my bathing suit yet." It was a long walk from the parking lot, through the woods, to the cabin. Who knew how long I would have to wait for my dad to walk all the way to the car and get back.

"Well, we can just walk to the water and put our feet in," my mother said. "Then we'll go for a real swim after lunch, how about that? All three of us."

The lake at the college retreat was man-made. It was dug out of the land to hold water for the reservoir, to hold water for all of New York City. It was clean, no seaweed and not too many fish, and not too deep at this end, and not very cold, not in August, anyway. And in this one spot, they had brought in sand and roped off a little swimming area. No one else was here.

My mom and I stood at the water's edge in our shorts and T-shirts. The sun had climbed well over the tops of the trees and perched there.

"Can't we swim now? *And* after lunch?" I asked my mom.

"Well, if we had waited for Daddy. But now you don't have your suit on, sweetie. And neither do I. But if you want to go in a little—not too far. I'll watch you from here."

I had done it many times. I always went in our backyard blow-up pool in just my underpants. I mean, of course I knew I was a girl but it hardly mattered back then. Boys were boys because they said so, but really, there was no difference. Just the month before, Brendon Harris, my next-door neighbor, and I came back from a long playground afternoon, and our mothers stripped us down to our underwear and sprayed us both with the garden hose. No biggie.

"Can I?" I asked my mother. The lake looked so good. It would cool me off. I wanted to put my face in the water and open my eyes. You could see the little rocks and sticks under the water in the sand, like a tiny, make-believe miniature world.

"Of course," my mother said. She was already pulling off my shirt and steadying my arm so I could step out of my shorts and flip-flops. "I'll be right here."

The sun spread across the skin of my bare shoulders like fire, like hot fingers. The sand whispered heat on the bottom of my feet. I walked carefully forward. The water was just warm enough, moving so slowly, letting my toes sink into the sand. And everywhere it was quiet. When I looked up at the sky, it was blue. When I looked back at my mom, she was watching me. Everything was just as it should be.

Until I heard voices. Voices talking the way you do when you think no one else is around. A family—I heard a mother and a father, and then a boy. The boy was complaining. He didn't want to be here, not at the lake. Not in a boat. Not at the college retreat at all. He did not like it here, he was saying, over and over.

I do not like Green Eggs and Ham.

I do not like them, Sam-I-am.

I froze.

I was naked in only my underpants. I had no shirt on. I may have only been five—or was I six already?—but I was suddenly naked, or half-naked, and it was horrible.

My body, which had just been warm and free and mine, was not anymore. I was petrified and more embarrassed than anything had ever made me feel before. And I was ashamed for having thought I could do this. Swim in my underwear. Out here in the wide world.

What was I thinking?

I couldn't turn around because that would be worse—I'd be facing them. I couldn't run back to our bags and grab a towel or my shirt.

How badly I wanted my shirt.

I knew enough to know that swimming out past my shoulders was, at best, a temporary solution. I'd have to come out eventually, or worse, that boy would come out here in the water too. How long could I hide in the murky green water?

I could hear the unfamiliar voices coming closer. I could

hear the mom telling the boy all the wonderful things about the retreat, the hikes, the campfires, s'mores, the fresh air. It wasn't working. I was getting nakeder and nakeder and for a full second it was like I could float out of my body and see myself standing by the water. I was a just a flat-chested little girl in big white cotton underpants. But I didn't feel like myself anymore.

Even as I felt my mother drape a towel around my shoulders, I knew I would never be the same again.

ten

Four o'clock was teatime at Mohawk. You can set your watch by it, Pam would tell us. She knew because she had to close up the gift shop between four and five fifteen every day. Mrs. Smith insisted. She didn't want anyone shopping or eating ice cream at teatime.

So then, just as the heat of the day is supposed to be waning but it feels hotter than ever, everyone comes inside to have hot tea and biscuits with homemade jam.

"We're not allowed in here," Eliza said. "So stay low."

I didn't really know what staying low meant, but I already knew that teatime was only for the guests. Aunt Louisa had told us many times not to bother Mrs. Smith—not to get underfoot— not to be using equipment, or taking up space, or doing anything that paying customers were paying to do.

And teatime at Mohawk was all Mrs. Smith.

I looked around. The littlest kids had escaped their parents' handholding and were crowding around the rolling tea cart, reaching between the legs of the grown-up guests and snatching sugar cookies from the tray. A couple of teenagers were milling as far apart from their parents as from each other, leaning against the walls of this huge carpeted room. The older people had gotten there early and taken most of the couches and settees and sofa chairs. Then they sent someone else to grab cookies for them so no one could take their seat. It was dark inside. The shades were drawn to keep the afternoon sun out.

"Try to blend in," Eliza instructed me.

Usually that was easy. Most of my life I feel like I blend in, or maybe I just don't stick out, which comes in pretty handy in school. There are some kids who always get in trouble; no matter who is talking, the teacher always looks at them first. And some kids that the teacher always relies on, and they are the ones who have to take things to the office or volunteer to read out loud or pass out papers. And then there are some kids who just get left alone. That was me.

So why did I feel different now?

I mean, why did I suddenly *want* to feel different?

Michael had chased us into the water, which caused my throat to produce a weird giggling laugh I never heard before. I almost forgot how to swim. I started moving my arms and legs but instead of feeling powerful, instead of flying through the water, I was flailing. Instead of feeling the freshness of the water on my skin I was fighting it. And all the while I sensed that Michael was right behind us. I could hear him breathing and splashing and my heart started thumping.

We all made it to the floating dock at the same time. Eliza hoisted herself up and then me and then Michael. We all flopped onto the wooden planks and stayed there. Nobody moved. No one stood up. No one talked. The dock still rocked, up and down from the weight of our bodies.

The dock was small and on the busiest days maybe six or seven guests could lay side by side like crayons melting in the sun. But even though we were the only ones there, Michael, Eliza, and I were all pretty close to each other, breathing hard. If there was a way to look comfortable, I tried to find it. I bent my knees just the slightest bit to lift my legs because for some reason I thought they looked better that way. But I was anything but comfortable.

I was anxious and uncomfortable and I had no idea what to say or do, but it was a good feeling. A new feeling. It wasn't like Christmas morning, but more like Christmas Eve when you are so excited, even scared-excited, that you won't get what you really wanted but maybe you will. Or that no one will like what you got for them. So flooded with tension you can't fall asleep, even knowing that falling asleep is the only way to make morning come. It's a feeling that you can't wait to get rid of, but I wanted to feel it again as soon as possible.

"Okay, so you're not chickens," Michael said. He leaned up on his elbows, water dripping from his head onto his shoulders.

That was a nice thing to say, I thought.

I should say something back. Something clever. Something really clever. Something to make me stand out—for once. So I don't blend in.

"You're just a jerk, Michael," Eliza said.

"Yeah, a dumb jerk," I added cleverly.

Most of the guests had dressed for teatime, put on pants and shirts. There was one man in a jacket. Some of the mothers had summer dresses and little low heels. But the kids looked pretty much the same. Like we did. Shorts. Wet hair. Flip-flops.

"Oh no," Eliza said, poking me in the side. "Why is he here?"

"Who?"

We had gotten close to the food table without being noticed. It was pretty crowded today. Mrs. Smith was circling around on the other side of the room, making sure everyone knew who she was. We could grab a cookie or five, a scone maybe, a handful of strawberries.

"Michael," Eliza whispered. "He never comes to teatime. He's gotten caught so many times his father would kill him if he finds out."

"He's here?"

"Yeah, now we better go or we'll all get in trouble."

He's here. And he never usually comes. But we are here. And he's here.

"C'mon," Eliza said. "Don't worry. I can get us stuff from the kitchen. Let's go. My dad will be mad too, if Mrs. Smith catches us. Michael always gets caught. He's got a sign around his neck or something. C'mon."

I tried to look around the room quickly but I didn't see him anywhere. Eliza pulled me through the side doors and onto the porch. Maybe it was just as well. If I had the opportunity to say one more clever thing today he might never want to talk to me again.

eleven

Mrs. Jaffe gave each of us—Peter and me—a note-book. The black-and-white kind that are so hard to write in and have pages that don't rip out. She told us it was for our feelings, the ones we might not want anyone else to know. She asked that we write in it at least once a week, and bring it to our once-a-month meetings with her.

But, she said, she would never read it. Never ask us to read it out loud. At the end of each meeting we had "quiet writing time" and we were supposed to write in it then, too. We were supposed to write about our parents, and the war, and what it felt like to worry if your mom or dad was going to live or die. Mrs. Jaffe didn't mince her words. No one else said things like that, like "war" or "die." It was scary but kind of a relief.

Spelling doesn't matter. Grammar and structure doesn't

matter. This isn't about school, Mrs. Jaffe told us. It's about listening to your own feelings. Owning them. Not being afraid of them.

I heard Peter make a sound under his breath. I thought it was dumb too, but I did it, every week, a little bit, and a little bit more. At the end of the school year, Mrs. Jaffe encouraged us to use our notebooks whenever we felt we needed to. And it did help. I wrote about my mom being in Iraq, about how much I missed her, and how many days until she was coming back. And for the longest time, that was all I wrote about in my journal.

Saturday was errand day. Usually Aunt Louisa let us stop at McDonald's and Uncle Bruce might let us rent a movie. Maybe two. Eliza and I always wanted to go into town.

"You can't stay alone, Julia," Eliza said. She even stamped her foot.

"Leave her alone, Liza," my Uncle Bruce said. "We all need to be alone sometimes. This is a small house—nobody gets to be alone too often. Now get your shoes on and let's go."

As soon as Aunt Louisa and Uncle Bruce and Eliza were gone, I took out my notebook. Maybe I was going write something about my mother, about missing her phone call for the second time in the same week. Or about the war, about missing limbs, or convoys or IEDs. No one should even have to know what an IED is, but I do. It's an improvised explosive device. I could have written about all those things, since they were on my mind, but I didn't. I wrote his name instead.

M-I-C-H-E-A-L.

I wish I knew his last name. I could write more, more letters to play with and decorate.

And then I wrote it again. *M-I-C-H-E-A-L*. And I wrote it again. I didn't even ask myself why I was doing this, I just was. Because, as I wrote his name, it was like he was closer to me. It was his name. It belonged to him, the letters filled the page, and little movies played in my head—almost without my permission— of how many different ways I might bump into Michael again. How could I make it happen? I had tried all week and the whole while I couldn't let Eliza know what I was doing.

Like on Wednesday.

"You don't even like horses, Julia," Eliza had said.

"I never said that. I like horses. All girls like horses, don't they?"

Black Beauty was one of my favorite books. And *Misty of Chincoteague.*

"You never did before."

"Well, I do now."

We were walking toward the stables. I figured if Michael's

father works here maybe Michael hangs out and helps him. And so far, Eliza was buying this. I was just glad she couldn't hear my heart thumping.

"Well, hold up your dress, then," Eliza said. "It's so dirty in there. Mother doesn't really want me doing things like that anymore. Remember?"

I looked down at my pinafore but it wasn't there. Usually it would be hanging just below my knees, brushing the tops of my boots. If everything was the same, I would be grateful not to be wearing a corset yet, grateful I could still breathe freely, run freely, and play. Not worrying about how ladylike I looked. Not like the fancy ladies who always look so weary, who don't walk but glide across the room and fan themselves slowly, in between sips of their tea.

But it wasn't the same anymore.

And Michael wasn't at the stables.

And then on Friday.

"Why don't we go swimming," I suggested and I wondered if Eliza could tell. Could she tell I wasn't wearing my swimming bloomers? That I didn't have my parasol. I hadn't been able to conjure up even a single sash, eyelet, or petticoat of muslin.

"Alas," Eliza said. "Off to our daily swim."

She couldn't tell, and Michael and his brother were at the lake. They were both on top of the log, their legs running in place, gripping it and letting it spin under their feet at the same time. They were facing each other, laughing. Michael didn't see us, see me.

"I don't want to stay here," Eliza said. I wasn't sure which Eliza was talking. Was it Olden-Day Eliza or just Eliza Eliza? But at that moment I didn't care any more than I had to in order to keep her next to me, long enough to be seen—by Michael.

The log was anchored on one end to the floating dock. The other end was tethered to a huge concrete slab on the shore. It was a famous tradition at Mohawk. Apparently it was an original log dating back to when the beach was first dug and the hotel first opened to the public.

"C'mon, Julia," Eliza said. "We can come swimming later."

Then I knew it was Eliza Eliza doing the talking, because Olden-Day Eliza would never say "c'mon."

Every fourth of July in the real olden days, before the picnic on the great lawn, the men—the guests and the employees—had log-spinning contests, while the women had to sit on wooden chairs, in high stockings, shoes, bathing dresses with long sleeves, and floppy wide-brimmed hats. And watch. Olden-Day Eliza and Julia could have stood on the beach and watched the festivities. Of course, girls weren't allowed to swim at the same time as the boys.

But Eliza was done trying to get me to pretend with her. She might not have figured it out completely but she knew I wasn't paying attention. And now she just wanted to go.

"We can catch a ride back with my dad," she told me. "If we leave now."

There wasn't really anything I could do, standing there in the sand, to get his attention. Let him know I was there—had sought him out, in fact. Though I wasn't sure if that would be a good thing or not. Probably not.

But I was finally there, after days of trying to figure out how to bump into him. I couldn't just leave now.

"Julia, c'mon." Eliza reached out her hand to me. She was just Eliza, my cousin, my niece, my best friend in sixth grade, in New Hope Middle School and for all my life. And I couldn't just let her down.

"Okay, we can go." I tried to say it loudly. In the end we caught our ride but I missed "bumping into" Michael whatever-his-last-name-was.

I wrote his name three more times—*M-i-c-h-e-a-l*. Michael. Michael—I wrote it in print and then script and then I closed my notebook.

Like Mrs. Jaffe told me—I was owning my feelings, whatever that meant.

twelve

I don't remember ever wanting to be alone with a boy. I sure never tried to be, but one afternoon for counseling, Mrs. Jaffe was late and for the longest time Peter Vos and I just sat there, at two opposite sides of the room.

"Maybe this is part of the program," I said out loud and for some reason Peter answered me.

"What is?" he said.

"This. This sitting here. Maybe we are supposed to write in our notebooks."

"So go ahead."

"Maybe we are supposed to talk to each other."

"Go blow," Peter said.

"That's not very nice," I said, wishing I had something meaner to say back, but I didn't.

It was quiet again.

"We should just go. I'm missing science again." I think that time I was just talking to myself.

Peter said, "Sorry."

"What?"

"Sorry. I didn't mean it. My dad's coming back."

"He is?"

"Yeah, next week sometime, they told us . . . ," Peter said.

"You must be happy."

Peter nodded but didn't offer anything more.

"So that's great." I tried not to sound jealous. I tried to make a joke. "You won't have to come to these sessions anymore."

"I'm scared," Peter said quietly, as if he wanted to tell me something but he also needed to keep it to himself.

So I pretended I hadn't heard.

They come in person. They come to your house in their full dress uniform and then you know. You know it's not good news. It's the worst news, so every day that you are home and you see someone in a uniform outside the window it takes you back for a minute. It takes your breath away for a moment or two.

Then you see it's the postman. Or the UPS man. Or even somebody in a navy blazer maybe that you caught out of the corner of your eye but didn't focus on and your heart freezes for just the split second. In the deployment program before my mom left, I heard about a kid who hid under his bed whenever he heard the doorbell ring. There was a girl who started hysterically crying this one time she got called to the principal's office. All they needed was to check on a field trip permission slip.

But I never thought I'd see them at Mohawk. The army. I never expected them to come all the way up here just to find me. To bring with them the news that is too awful to write down in a letter.

There were three of them, walking up the hill nearing the rose trellises. It was early. How did they get here so early? For once, Eliza and I woke up when Uncle Bruce did and we got a ride with him to the hotel. It was my idea. I didn't wonder why the army had come to Mohawk instead of my house. I didn't think.

I've got to run away, I thought.

They were coming closer. Navy blue, bright white, bright red.

My brain started spinning. *Eliza and I can hang out by the lake all day. We can swim or take out a boat, and either way I can keep an eye on the beach, keep a lookout. I can make sure the soldiers never find me. If they never find me they can't tell me. If they can't tell me that means nothing bad has happened.*

"Julia, what's wrong? What's the matter?"

I had thought every day that this could happen, that this

might happen—but I didn't think they should be laughing like that. *Why are they laughing?*

Eliza was pulling at my arm. "Julia, it's a wedding. What are you looking at?"

The whole thing had lasted ten seconds, if that. In ten seconds my brain flew out of my body, traveled all the way around the world, broke in two, and now I was back to normal. Just like that.

Like nothing had ever happened.

It was a wedding. There were always weddings at Mohawk, practically every weekend. The groom, or maybe it was the bride's family, must have had someone in the military. The whole wedding party was coming over the hill, smiling and laughing and starting to group together. The photographer was telling everyone where to stand.

thirteen

An entire hall at the far end, at the top of the carpeted stairs, was roped off with a red velvet cord. The rope hung, swaying heavy in the middle with age. It was hardly even red anymore. That's where Mrs. Smith lived and it was forbidden to go down that hall or anywhere near those rooms. They were private.

It was our favorite place to wander.

"Are you sure she's not here now?"

"She's gone," Eliza said to me. "She's always at the lunch service."

We liked it down there because it was empty. We would never encounter someone smelling of suntan lotion, wearing a pair of Juicy shorts, iPod earphones, or hoodies. We would never hear the modern voices of swearing teenagers or whining children.

It was the end of July and hot outside. I had talked to my mother last night and she told me she'd be home soon. She couldn't tell me the exact date because she didn't know or they wouldn't let her say. But soon, she promised. A month from now. Four weeks. Five, tops.

By the end of August.

She promised.

Meanwhile young ladies had to stay indoors in such hot weather as this, so they wouldn't glisten. Eliza told me that's what they called sweating in the olden days and we shouldn't do it. It's unbecoming of a lady, Eliza said.

I should know—or I should pretend I know—what "unbecoming" means and if things were working like they used to, it wouldn't matter. Eliza and I would be playing together and inside that world, we would both know. But now its like there's a tiny part of me that is standing outside, in the real world, with one foot holding the door open. When I am all sweaty, from summer, and from running—do boys think it's "unbecoming"? Would Michael?

So I have to figure out what unbecoming means, and I decide it's not pretty. It's not attractive to be sweating. Not on your face, or behind your knees, or down your back, and certainly not under your arms. I tried to walk more slowly so I wouldn't work up a sweat.

There were more old photographs hanging here in this hall than anywhere else all over the hotel. Silent faces in black and white staring out of the frames. Barely anyone smiled. If there was more than one person in the picture, they were either standing or sitting upright or a combination. Sometimes a man and woman together. She was sitting. He was standing. There were grown men with long sideburns, and women always wearing white. There were only a few photographs of children.

As we walked farther down the hall the photographs got newer, if you could call them that. Some were even in color, but most of them still formal and posed.

"Look at this one." Eliza stopped and pointed.

"Who's that?"

"I don't know. But she's really pretty, isn't she?"

I looked closely at the face, wondering what makes someone pretty or not. Was I pretty? I mean, my dad always said so, but that didn't really count. My mom counted even less. I looked at Eliza. She looked okay. She looked fine. There was nothing unpretty about her.

Was she pretty?

I knew there were some girls who got told they were pretty all the time. By teachers, by other grown-ups. By strangers. Like Jody Reynolds. Jody had really long, curly blond hair and a round face. She was tiny. *What a pretty girl you are,* people were always saying. I heard it all the time, because I'd ridden the bus with her since kindergarten. *You look so pretty today, Jody. You are such a pretty girl.*

I don't remember anyone other than family saying that about Eliza. Or me.

I looked back at the girl in the photograph. She must have been about fourteen or fifteen years old. She was standing in front of an old car like from the drive-in movie days. She was wearing a full skirt and a tight sweater tucked neatly inside. Her hair was dark and her lips were smiling. You could even see the thick curl of her eyelashes in the picture. Are those the things that make someone pretty?

"Do you think I'm pretty?"

"What?" Eliza asked.

It surprised me, too. But what I really wanted to know, I suppose, was if Michael thought I was pretty. As if suddenly, that's all that mattered.

Does Michael whatever-his-last-name-is think that I'm pretty?

"Nothing," I told Eliza. "Forget it."

Worrying if a boy thinks you are pretty or not is like standing on the beach and realizing you are wearing nothing but your underwear.

There isn't much you can do about it.

fourteen

One woman was killed during the three-day battle at Gettysburg in the Civil War. She was in her house baking bread when a stray bullet from one of the soldiers shot through the side of her house and hit her in the back. Mohawk would have just begun to be built. The foundation poured. The quarries dug. The long road just being cut through the thick woods heading straight up the mountain.

The dark floral carpet would have not yet have been laid. The stone watchtower not yet finished. There is a picture in the hall of little five-year old Clara Sidney Smith, Mrs. Smith's grand-mother, standing in the center of the deep concrete well before it was opened and water flooded it to the top. She is wearing a white sailor suit and matching hat, white stockings and white boots and staring into the camera without a care in the world.

The date on the photograph says May 15, 1869—just four years after the end of the Civil War. The last war to be fought on United States soil.

When my mother first went away to Iraq, I cried every single night. My stomach hurt and I couldn't eat. I went to bed really early, but I couldn't sleep and I would get up in the middle of the night and go on my computer. Even my dad didn't know. It was dark in my room but the glow from my computer was like a little heartbeat.

I would go online hoping to see an e-mail from my mother. And then I would log off and on again a second later because I knew it was daytime in Iraq and she might have written just at that second. Or maybe it took a little while in cyberspace to get here and if I signed on and off it would appear. But when it didn't it would make my stomach hurt even more.

And sometimes while I was waiting to see if an e-mail would suddenly appear I would search online. I would plug in keywords like "Women in war," "nurses," and "wartime." "History of women in the military." Maybe it took a while for e-mail to travel across time zones, and over oceans and across nighttime skies.

But my mother still wouldn't be there in the morning to make my breakfast. And I knew she wouldn't be there when I got dressed and left for school. And she wouldn't be there when I got home again.

Those first few months were horrible. It was like being home-sick but worse. I didn't do my homework but nobody said anything. I spent all day in school trying not to think about where my mom was, what she might be doing or seeing.

My dad and I did everything we could to avoid the news but sometimes there would be a commercial for it while we were watching our sitcom. Breaking news. Or stay tuned for News at Ten, as if hearing about people getting killed or hurt would make you want to watch it. Then we'd hear something about a roadside bomb or the number of casualities since the war started, before we could find the controller and change the channel. They might even break it down by number of men, women, civilians, and army personnel.

Three hundred and thirty. Four hundred and two. Seven hundred and sixty-four dead.

Then one day I just forgot. I was watching my shows and my dad and I were eating dinner in front of the TV. I had a fork-ful of my chicken potpie all the way up to my mouth and it was funny. It was so funny, something that happened in the show was funny and I laughed. We both laughed. Not just a smile or a little chuckle but me and Dad were laughing out loud so when the commercial came on, at first, we didn't hear it. We were still laughing.

I think I remember. Someone had fallen down, hit on the head with a plank of wood, slipped and fell into a hole, that kind of funny. The funny you shouldn't be laughing at in the first place, but you do. Partly because you are so glad it's not you, and then because people look so funny when they fall down.

"The number of American casualties since the start of the war has reached one thousand," the reporter said. She was looking right at me, out of the TV. It was a milestone. Like an important birthday or anniversary. Like all the others were child's play. They didn't really count. This is the big one. One thousand Americans have been killed in Iraq. They are dead and will never come back home to watch TV with their kids, or their mom, or their brother. It was newsworthy.

And we were laughing.

When I think about that lady who got shot in the battle of Gettysburg I wonder if she had any kids. I mean, who else would she be baking that bread for? What a way to die. But it doesn't matter now. Nobody has even heard of her. Nobody even knows her name.

fifteen

ester and Lynette belonged to a long line of other "Villiators," dolls who lived in the doll village or "D'Ville." D'Ville was really a huge plastic bin filled to the top with all sorts of dolls in all degrees of newness, from brand-new to downright legless and armless, even headless, stages. But every single one of them, collected over all the years Eliza and I had been playing together, had a name. Not only a first but also a last name, a family, a hobby, and a talent.

When we were really little we used to line them all up, or divide them into groups. There was the hair color camp, where they had talent shows divided into teams by the color of their hair. There was the tease-y group that used to mean girls but now it was just the older kids, not quite grown-up dolls, the ones we didn't know where else to put. The tease-y group got to do the most things, go to camp. Go to college. Have singing contests. Usually I got to be the dolls in the tease-y group.

It was only a couple of years ago that we stopped needing the dolls themselves to play. It was almost as if we ourselves had become characters in D'Ville. We carried them within us. Lester and Lynette were the only two characters that weren't real dolls. They lived in D'Ville but they were us.

Eliza and I were Lester and Lynette.

Or at least we used to be.

Before I *used* them, like I did today, to get Eliza to stay up at the hotel with me.

I kept hoping we would see Michael, but I never told Eliza that. Instead I told Eliza I wanted to play Lester and Lynette so we could hang around a little longer. We never did "bump" into Michael or his brother, but we missed our ride home with Uncle Bruce and by the time we started walking home I just didn't feel like even pretending to pretend anymore.

"You never wanted to play Lester and Lynette, did you?" Eliza accused me after about half a mile.

"Yes, I did," I defended myself, because I wasn't really lying, was I? I *did* like playing. I thought I did. I sometimes did. So why not now? But Eliza could feel it. "I'm just tired now. From walking."

"It was *your* idea to walk," Eliza said. "Now I have this huge blister on my foot. And it hurts."

"That's not *my* fault."

"Well, it's sure not *my* fault. We wouldn't be walking if we had left when *I* wanted to," Eliza said.

"Oh, you had that blister a long time ago," I said, because I felt guilty.

"No, I didn't," Eliza said. "I just got. I'm just getting it now because we are walking so much and my sock has a hole in it."

"Well, jeez, it's sure not my fault you put on hole-ly socks." And I made myself feel better.

When we got home, Eliza had to wash her feet and then put a big Band-Aid on her heel and a little blood even soaked right through that. Now Aunt Louisa was snoring again but Eliza was fast asleep and I wasn't. Far away I could hear the roll of thunder like the earth letting us know it was unhappy. Then the room was alive in a flash of warm light with no sound at all. Heat lightning my mother would call that. I slipped out of bed.

Back in our house in town, when a storm was coming, my mother and I would go out and sit on the screened-in porch, waiting for the rain, counting the seconds between the bolt of light and the scary thunder. *One thousand one. One thousand two. One thousand three* and when the moment between the light and the sound was indistinguishable, we knew the storm was right on top of us. Hard rain would pummel the roof of our house, and the lightning would shake the floor and walls when it hit, so close.

We were safe inside, only the warm, wet wind could touch us, blow our hair and dampen our faces. I would sit on my mother's lap, holding her tight, pretending to be scared.

But now I was alone. I stood in the grass looking up at the night. And I was afraid. The storm was coming closer, I could hear it. When the lightning came, it lit up the whole world completely, so for a split second it was daylight. Like it was in Iraq right now.

And I couldn't say for sure, at that very moment, if my mother was alive or dead. Wounded or working. Or resting. Or getting ready for her day. She said she felt like she could never get all the sand out of her hair.

I lifted my arms and tried to glide like an angel. The wind was picking up. I could hear, even in the dark, the way the trees sounded different, leaves brushing up against one another in warning. A musky smell rose up from the ground.

I should go inside, I thought. But I didn't want to.

"It's beautiful right before a storm, isn't it, Julia?" Uncle Bruce's voice was so distinct, like the sound of his truck over the gravel driveway, rough and familiar.

He stood next to me on the grass and looked up. He didn't ask me what I was doing out here in the middle of the night.

"Yeah," I said.

I wondered if he knew Eliza was mad at me. He must have

noticed that neither one of us had spoken one word all through dinner.

"We sure need the rain," he said.

I looked up again at the sky and I felt like I was about to cry. Uncle Bruce took one step toward me and put his arm around my shoulders.

"She's going to be all right, Julia, and so are you," he said. "Everything's going to be fine."

The thunder rumbling in the distance began to sound closer. I let myself lean against Uncle Bruce. His body blocked the wind and we stood that way until he said we should go in. And then, just after I crawled back into bed next to Eliza, who was still fast asleep, the rain began and when it did, it poured.

All during breakast, Eliza kept her focus on her Fruity Pebbles, so I knew she was still upset with me, although Aunt Louisa didn't seem to notice. She kept chatting away like nobody's business.

"Did it rain last night? It must have rained all night. Did anyone else hear that rain last night?"

Aunt Louisa got up from the table to start her chores. Five loads of laundry, she said. That's a lot of dirty clothes. Then she sat down to watch TV. Uncle Bruce had long since left for work.

A part of me didn't want anything to do with Eliza right now. She didn't have to pout like this and let everybody know. And besides, I was tired of always being grouped together, always and forever. Julia and Eliza. Eliza and Julia.

And another part of me was lonely. For Eliza and for when

I used to be nice. I remembered when we were both little, Eliza couldn't tell the difference between animation and living characters on the TV. She couldn't tell you if SpongeBob was real or a cartoon. Or if Lizzy McGuire was animated or alive. At first no one would believe me.

"She doesn't know. She really doesn't," I would say. And then everyone started grilling her with names.

"Power Rangers?" Uncle Bruce asked her.

"Living?" Eliza would try and she was serious.

I gave her one. "Lilo and Stitch."

"Living?"

And we would all laugh, especially Eliza. I think she loved the attention but I knew she really couldn't tell the difference.

"Harry Potter?" my mother would ask.

"Animated?"

I was lonely for Eliza. So out of the blue I just said, "Shrek."

Nothing.

"Raven," I tried another one. *That's So Raven* was one of Eliza's favorite shows.

She looked up. I saw a little smile, the tiniest smile showing.

"Animated?"

I knew she was playing with me. I knew it was going to be okay.

seventeen

A nd Peter's father did come back, just before the end of school—only a couple of months after he had left for his second tour.

"Do you want to talk about it?" Mrs. Jaffe was asking.

No, I thought. *Why would he want to talk about it? He hasn't talked all year.*

But he did.

Nonstop. All of a sudden Peter Vos was a virtual chatterbox.

"They sent him home early," Peter told us.

It was just the three of us in the room, like always. It was a half-day kindergarten room, the room we used when the half-day kindergarten kids all got to go home. I felt huge sitting in those tiny chairs at that tiny table. There were gigantic colorful pictures of the alphabet all around the room. Colors, and numbers, and the seasons—winter, spring, summer, fall. And faces of the clock, faces, real faces all pointing to different times. The hour and the half hour. All smiling. All cartoons, nothing real.

"He got hurt but not really hurt. Not hurt in his body, anyway," Peter went on. "He didn't get his face blown off, or his brains blown out, or anything like that, either."

I shuddered, all the way from my shoulders to my toes. No one ever talked that way. But Mrs. Jaffe was nodding her head and listening, sitting right under the ridiculously gleeful face whose nose had hands pointing to twelve noon.

"He's different now. My dad is different."

"How so?" Mrs. Jaffe asked him.

"He's angry all the time," Peter said. "He yells. He likes it quiet in the house. When my baby sister started running around the kitchen, making all this noise, he slammed his fist down on the counter. He told her to shut up."

I saw that Peter wasn't looking at Mrs. Jaffe when he was talking. He wasn't looking at me, either. His head was turned and his eyes were looking up at the ceiling. It was like he didn't want anyone to connect him to what he was saying.

"Kaley's two and a half," Peter said. "She doesn't understand. And he screams. At night. In his sleep, I guess."

I felt bad for Peter, I did. But in that moment all I could think of was my mom. My mom crying or screaming. Or coming home so different. Did that happen to everyone?

"He's always angry," Peter went on.

"Does he talk to you about it, Peter?" Mrs. Jaffe was saying. "Or your mom?"

Peter shook his head. "Nobody talks about anything."

Mrs. Jaffe leaned closer to him. "This is the place to talk, Peter," she said.

Peter finally lowered his eyes. He looked at her and I couldn't tell if he was really sad or really mad and he said, "Well, sometimes I wish my dad hadn't come home at all."

eighteen

My dad was supposed to take me home every weekend and bring me back Sunday night so he could go to work again Monday. But last weekend my dad called and said he had to work and Aunt Louisa said it was easier having me around anyway, which made me feel kind of good about that, but sad that I wouldn't get to see my dad.

Now the weekend had come again and I didn't want to go.

I wanted to go up to the hotel, which we didn't usually do on weekends. First of all, Uncle Bruce liked to stay home on his days off, and second, weekends were the busiest at Mohawk and Mrs. Smith didn't like us "underfoot." But sometimes, maybe, there was always a chance, I thought. If I wanted it badly enough I could find a way to get up to the mountain house.

Michael would be there, I bet.

There was the Saturday night outdoor movie on the lawn. I bet he would be there, at the movie. I imagined the sun would have just set and crowds of people would be gathering around in the almost dark summer evening. *Oh, hi*, I might have said as if I barely remembered who he was.

Or maybe I would just nod my head like I knew but didn't really care.

"Your dad's here," Eliza shouted and she ran to open the door.

I felt my hopes sink.

"Okay, I probably should have told you before," Aunt Louisa said, getting to her feet. "Dad's here to visit, Julia, but he's not going to be able to take you for the weekend."

I looked over at my dad who was now standing inside. He had his hands in his pockets. Aunt Louisa seemed to be doing the talking for him as if they had it all planned out.

"Well, Dad has to work again, the weekend shift. And it's no big deal, but summer is good overtime and it will just make it easier when your mom comes home and all."

My dad said, "I'm sorry, sweetie, but let's have a good visit while I'm here."

So many thoughts jumped into my brain one at a time, so fast they collided.

First: *Oh, goody, I can go up to the mountain house.*

Second: *But we're not supposed to go to the mountain house on weekends.*

Third: *Maybe I can figure out a way*—then fourth: *I am not going home this weekend and it's been a month* and that's when I started to feel really bad.

"Now, Julia." My dad put his arms around me. "It's only another week."

I pressed my face into my dad's shirt. I had never felt more homesick. How could I have wanted something so badly a second ago that was making me feel awful now? How could I be so sad and so excited all at the same time?

"C'mon now, everyone. We have lots of time," Aunt Louisa said. "Who wants something to drink? Some chips?"

When Uncle Bruce came home we all ate dinner together, and when my mom called even she seemed to know I wasn't going home for the weekend. I was the only one who didn't get any say in my own life.

"I love you, Julia. I miss you like crazy," she told me.

I couldn't hear her that well and besides there was no privacy so I just acted like everything was fine, even though I felt so uncomfortable inside.

"I miss you, too, Mommy," I said. I sounded like a baby and

I knew everybody at the table was listening to me and for some reason that made me so mad.

When it was time for my dad to leave, Aunt Louisa and I walked him out to his car. Every step closer I got madder and madder and then I started to cry. I couldn't help it, it all just came out.

My dad turned around. "Sweetie, please, don't make me feel worse than I already do." He took a few steps toward the front seat of his car and then he reached into the backseat. "Look, sweetie, your mom and I were going to give you this when she gets back in a couple of weeks, but now seems like a better time."

He handed me a cell phone.

Louisa gripped her hands together and it made a clapping sound. "Wow, Julia, look at that. How exciting."

I had wanted a cell phone for so long, but somehow right now it just seemed wrong.

"Don't you like it?" my dad asked.

I did. "I do," I said. I was stuck in the middle of myself again and neither side was very pretty. If I took the cell phone it made me look selfish and if I didn't I looked ungrateful.

It was pink.

"It's all set up." My dad smiled. He looked happier.

"Thanks, Dad." I sniffled.

• • •

Louisa and I stood in the driveway and watched our dad head off down the road. He had a bumper sticker of two yellow ribbons on either side of the bold printed words: SUPPORT OUR TROOPS. I remembered when we bought it, at the pharmacy in town, just after my mom left for Iraq.

nineteen

By Saturday morning I had pretty much replaced my homesickness by hatching the perfect plot for getting Eliza to agree see the movie with me up at Mohawk. Well, actually I had no plan yet at all, but I was mentally hard at work on it until Aunt Louisa just crushed my dreams like a bug on the windowsill.

"No one's going up to the hotel over the weekend," Aunt Louisa said. "You two can occupy yourselves right here."

Really, life should have an accompanying soundtrack. There should be pathetic violin music playing just in case you are not sure how you are going to feel. But I knew. The disappointment washed over me as quickly as I could understand the words coming from her mouth. I felt like a wall had just fallen down on me, crushing me and all my potential plans underneath.

But sometimes it's better not to show your hand. And most times it's better not to show your handwriting, either. Eliza was fine with not going up to the hotel, but I went to hide in the bathroom because that's what a journal is for.

I wrote: *M-i-c-h-e-a-l. M-i-c-h-e-a-l.* And when I was too embarrassed to read over my own sentences, the ones I had just written, I just kept writing.

I have to get up to the hotel tonight. I have to be there if Michael shows up for the outdoor movie. He's got to show up. He's just got to. And Aunt Louisa has to let me go. She's not my mother. She can't tell me what to do anyway.

Uncle Bruce knocked on the bathroom door. "Are you all right in there, Julia?"

"I'm fine."

I listened as his footsteps moved away. But there was only one bathroom in the house, so I had to write fast before someone had to use the toilet.

Michael is the one. I think I really like him. And if I can just see him alone I will know for sure. Movie night is my only chance. I've got to find a way to get up there. Summer is already half over and I won't have the chance ever again. I don't know where he goes to school. I don't even know his last name!!!!

My life was terrible.

Then, just like that, the background music changed.

Aunt Louisa and Uncle Bruce had to drive all the way up to Albany to pick up the truck from a friend who did the work at cost, which meant it would cost a lot less on this end. And they had to go today or else at four thirty Monday morning in order to be back in time for Uncle Bruce to get to work.

"I don't want to leave you girls alone," Aunt Louisa was saying and Eliza was whining about how she didn't want to drive a whole two hours just to turn around and drive back again.

"I stay alone all the time," I added, knowing that four hours would be just what I needed.

"Mom, we'll be fine. You've left me alone before. And besides," Eliza added. "We're not alone. We have each other."

Inside, my heart was pounding with the anticipation that Eliza would be able to convince her mom to go without us, even though I knew we had completely different reasons. And even though I knew I wasn't being fair by keeping mine a secret.

"Well, okay," Aunt Louisa gave in.

I swear, if there was an orchestra playing somewhere, it would be getting louder and louder, building up to that moment just before the girl meets the boy—

—And then they kiss.

twenty

Even while Eliza was explaining why never in a million years would she agree to sneak out and walk up to the hotel, I was imagining how I would first see Michael. What it would be like. What I would say. What he would say.

Uncle Bruce and Aunt Louisa pulled out of the driveway, but not before telling us they would be back in a few hours. *Don't let anyone in. Don't answer the phone unless you hear someone you know talking into the machine.*

And don't go anywhere.

"It's not somewhere," I was telling Eliza. "It's practically still staying home."

"But it's not, Julia."

"But no one will know."

"C'mon. It will be fun," I told Eliza. "Like we are runaway slaves."

"Following the North Star," Eliza added.

"Or we were captured by Indians and now we have to walk for miles back to their camp so they can adopt us into their tribe."

"They live in a longhouse."

"And the clan mother hands us each a cornhusk doll to represent our new family."

We headed up to the hotel, promising our Olden-Day selves that we'd be back before the "high moon rises," or something like that.

The peepers were so loud, almost desperate. The sun was resting along the tops of the trees and spreading a golden light across the road. It was already late enough in the summer that the days were noticeably shorter and there was a coolness at night that hinted at the start of autumn. The movie would start as it was just beginning to be dark so the little kids could stay up and watch. There would be a later movie too for the grown-ups only, but I knew we'd have to get back before then.

I could hear the right words coming out of my mouth: moccasins, wampum beads, canoe. I could hear the story we were telling, but the whole walk up to the hotel I was only hoping beyond hope that Michael would be there early too.

twenty-one

It was seven thirty and still light, a gray light, but the movie had started. A couple of Mohawk employees in their green polo shirts were making popcorn in a giant hot-air popcorn machine, scooping it into paper bags, and handing them out to anyone who wanted one. For free.

Chairs had been set up in rows all along the great lawn and the movie was projected onto a giant screen that rose up against the stone guest-room side of the hotel. There were big black speakers on either side, and a papery rug rolled out between aisles. But no Michael.

"I wonder if they had popcorn in the olden days." Eliza was talking. "They had the corn. I wonder if they just popped it one day, like by accident or something, and then someone ate it and

said, umm yummy. But I guess the Iroquois wouldn't have butter, right? I wonder if they had salt."

My eyes were scanning the people in the seats, soaking in all
the remaining light, trying to make out the figures, the groups of
kids and teenagers, parents. He wasn't next to that old man in
the front row with the jacket, was he?

"Julia, are you listening? Do you want to sit here or not?"
Eliza was pointing to the empty last row. "No one will notice us
here and we can leave early."

"Fine," I said.

"I'll get us some popcorn," Eliza said. She slipped off and I
plopped down in the folding chair, my heart sinking.

"Thought you might be here."

I turned around and it was Michael. It was him. Right next to
me. His whole body, his face. Everything looked sort of muted in
the dusk, with the light from the screen, like a movie in a movie.
I struggled to keep my brain working. My body had already
betrayed me; my breathing was too fast, and I could feel an odd
sensation rise to the surface of my skin. I shivered.

"You cold?" Michael asked me. "It gets colder up here at
night than down in town. The mountains, I think."

"No," I said but as soon as the words came out of my mouth
I wondered if I should have answered differently. Had that

sounded unfriendly? Did it sound like I wanted to be left alone?

I didn't.

I had planned this exactly. It was an imaginary story and it had come true and now I didn't know what to do.

"I mean, I'm fine. Are you cold?" I said. I looked at his face and then looked away.

"Me? I'm never cold."

The sounds of the movie, the chill starting to replace the heat in the air, the grays of light and shadow. The grass under my feet was damp with wetness seeping into my sandals. I could feel that he was next to me as if some power in the universe had made this happen.

But Eliza would be back any minute. And all this would be over.

"I have a cell phone," I said suddenly.

Did that sound like I was bragging? Did that sound like I wanted him to call me? Did he even hear me?

"Yeah, so? I have one too," Michael answered, reaching into his back pocket.

I didn't know what to say now.

Then Michael asked, "So what's the number? I'll call you and you'll have my number too."

It was like my heart squeezed into a little ball, exploded, and flooded my body. Michael plugged in the number as I gave it to him. My cell phone vibrated almost instantaneously. He flipped his phone shut and it stopped but his number appeared on my screen.

"Maybe I can call you then sometime?" he asked me.

I nodded.

"Or text you?"

I shrugged. "Whatever."

I thought I was surely getting better at this by the minute.

By the time Eliza returned, Michael had left. I could barely let the popcorn touch my mouth. I wasn't hungry at all. I stared at the big screen and the flickering images but I don't remember what the movie was about. When Eliza said we should probably start heading back, I agreed. There were no cars on the road and it was completely dark. We couldn't see the hotel behind us anymore and I could barely see the road ahead of us. We started to run.

twenty-two

I saw Peter later that same day, the same day he told Mrs. Jaffe and me that his dad had come home, come home different. I saw him on the playground with his friends. I recognized one of the other boys that Peter was throwing a ball around with. He lived on the same street as I did but I didn't really *know* any of Peter's friends. He was in the sporty group, all boys who played Pop Warner football in the fall and did Little League in the spring. Alexandra Joyce was the only girl in that group and only because she could pitch and they had to let her on the team.

But even Alexandra Joyce didn't get to play ball during recess.

Peter looked up when Eliza and I walked by the patch of grass next to where the boys were playing. He didn't talk much to me outside of Mrs. Jaffe's room and I knew after today he probably wanted to forget everything he had said. I knew I would. But I waved my fingers at him and he waved back. Then when I was almost out of earshot I heard Peter shouting out to one of his friends. I could hear the grunt in his voice so I knew he was the one throwing the ball. Far, as hard as he could. He called out loudly, "What do Baghdad and Hiroshima have in common?"

I stopped and looked back.

"I don't know." The boy caught the ball, lifted his arm, and threw.

"Nothing," Peter paused, ball in hand, and then shouted, "Yet."

I knew what Hiroshima was. It was the Japanese city that was bombed and completely destroyed by the Americans in 1945. Almost every website about the end of World War II had the same photo of a woman whose shirt was burned right into her body and it left a geometric tattoo on her skin.

It took me a second to get it. Peter was telling a joke.

"That's a funny one, Pete." The other boy laughed but I don't think he even understood what it meant.

Eliza pulled me away, but not before I saw Peter look at me, to see if I had heard.

twenty-three

We had practically run the whole way home. Eliza lifted her arms like wings and let the wind carry her up into the air but I had already forgotten what we used to see. If Eliza really had feathers, I would have seen them falling off, one by one and being carried into the night sky. But of course, she didn't. She didn't really have wings, did she?

I ran right beside her with my hands out too. It felt good. I let the excitement of the night flood through me.

"We're flying." Eliza laughed.

"We can look down on the whole world," I said even though I couldn't. "I can see our school."

"I can see the playground."

"I can see Tomasello Pool."

And Eliza was happy.

We were both lying in bed but not nearly asleep when we heard Uncle Bruce and Aunt Louisa come back.

"They could have called when we weren't here," Eliza suddenly whispered to me. "What if my mom called the house and we didn't pick up?"

It seized the inside of my chest. What if she had?

How could I not have thought of that?

"There's nothing we can do about it now," I said. I kept my eyes on the wall but when Aunt Louisa pulled open the screen, I shut them as quickly as I could.

"Are you sleeping, girls?" Aunt Louisa said quietly. I could tell she was leaning over the bed. She said it again. Eliza rustled and groaned and shifted onto her side.

I felt terrible. Aunt Louisa would be so angry at Eliza if she thought we had left the house. She might punish Eliza for the rest of the summer. But she wouldn't be able to do anything to me. She never did.

Eliza always got the blame when I was here. It was like Aunt Louisa was afraid of upsetting me. I could hear Eliza breathing steadily as if she were fast asleep.

How did she do that?

I squeezed my eyes shut. At least I was facing the wall but I couldn't hold my breath much longer.

Finally, Aunt Louisa pulled the covers over our shoulders

and left the room. I heard the screen slide across the floor and click into place. The TV sounds came on, the gray light moved across the ceiling, from light to dark, and dark to light, like a moth was batting against a bare bulb.

"She would have said something if she knew," Eliza said. "She would have asked."

I let out my breath. Aunt Louisa wasn't the secretive type. If we were in trouble we would know by now. The heat pressed down on the sheet, on my legs. I inched my feet out the bottom and let out my breath.

We had gotten away with it.

I had gotten away with it.

So why did I feel so guilty?

twenty-four

Marion Crandell was the first American woman to be killed in World War I and she wasn't even a soldier. Or a nurse. She was a French teacher from Iowa and she was working in a YMCA kitchen giving out food to French soldiers. The place where she was working—dishing out beans, maybe cole slaw, maybe pork?—was hit by a German artillery shell only two months after she got there.

And she was killed.

On March 29, 1918, there was a small mention from the Associated Press from Paris. The headline read: AMERICAN WOMAN KILLED.

Pam always kept a bench piled with newspapers by the door to her gift shop. Sometimes guests requested a particular paper be delivered for the week of their stay. But she always had *The New York Times* and *The Wall Street Journal* and I always avoided looking at them.

"Hi, girls," Pam greeted us. "Hot enough for you?" She was fanning herself with a magazine. It was early. Monday morning, the hotel was still quiet and mostly empty. Voices were low. Eliza and I had gotten a ride with Uncle Bruce. After a whole Sunday of doing nothing, even Eliza was anxious to get out of the house.

"Yup," Eliza answered. "It's hot enough."

"Maybe you two could take a paddle boat out. Before the guests get up," Pam suggested.

"Yeah, let's do that," I said, poking around the gifts and souvenirs.

Eliza looked at me. "But just a second ago you said you didn't feel like it."

She was right. I had nixed every idea Eliza had come up with if I didn't think it would somehow increase our chances of running into Michael. But now it seemed like a good idea. Besides, it would use up time until lunch, I thought—until Michael was done working in the stables. He told me he helped his dad every morning before lunch and then the rest of the day was his. He was free. He always went swimming in the afternoons. That I knew already. I made sure Eliza and I had our bathing suits on under our shorts.

"Well, now I do. Do you feel like it?" I asked Eliza. I put down the glass globe with the miniature version of the hotel inside and turned back to the counter.

I didn't want to glance at the newspapers. But there it was.

US MILITARY DEATHS IN IRAQ WAR AT 1,486

At first it didn't even make sense. The number was so big, so huge. I couldn't imagine one thousand people. I couldn't imagine five hundred. It was hard to see a hundred people in my mind at once. There were twenty-three kids in my class last year. Eighty in the grade. Two hundred and fifty in the whole school.

What did one thousand, four hundred and eighty-six feel like? Sound like? One thousand, four hundred and eighty-six pine coffins? One thousand, four hundred and eighty-six American flags? More than a thousand empty spaces at the dinner table. Tens of thousands of books left unread? Millions of pieces of clothing, shoes, and gloves left in closets. What happened to all that stuff?

It was too much.

No brain could hold that all. No one could see all those faces, and shoes, and dinner plates, bedtime stories, and kisses.

So I didn't.

It was just a huge, ridiculous number and so it meant nothing to me at all. Was I still staring at the newspaper?

US MILITARY DEATHS IN IRAQ WAR AT 1,486

No, it didn't even register.

Eliza looked at Pam and Pam looked at me. But I had gotten used to not seeing things that were right in front of my face.

I was fine.

"So is it too early for ice cream?" Pam said, maybe a little more loudly than she needed to.

I picked a Fudgesicle from the freezer because it felt most like breakfast since we hadn't eaten anything yet. Eliza was about to take the same thing until I reminded her not to be a copycat and she took a vanilla Drumstick, which looked like the better choice after all but I couldn't change my mind now. I'd look like a baby.

"Thanks, Pam," Eliza said.

"Thanks," I echoed and I held the door for Eliza to go first.

The gift shop was air-conditioned but the hotel itself was not. And it had been cool outside early this morning when Uncle Bruce was ready to leave—we both wore sweatshirts—but already the air in the hallway was still and warm. Our ice creams seemed to feel the heat first and instantly soften.

"It's going to be a scorcher," Eliza said as she peeled the paper from her cone and stuffed it into her pocket.

"I'll say." I balled my wrapper up at the bottom of my Fudgesicle to catch the dripping.

You could smell the olden days coming from the wallpaper and the wooden floors, holding on to the years like memories.

We walked and licked and talked and licked.

Then as we headed through the main hall, past the check-in counter, Eliza tried to take her sweatshirt off over her head while holding her cone in one hand at a time. She almost had it, but the phone rang at the desk, and when I stopped suddenly—because phone ringing always startles me—Eliza banged into me and the top of her cone landed right on the floor between the two of us. It started melting into the carpet immediately.

So if I look back now I see all the little events that, if they had just gone another way, or occurred a second or two later, or a second or two earlier, would have made all the difference. If I hadn't made that comment about being a copycat—Fudgsicles are much more stable than ice-cream cones. Or if the phone hadn't rung at right that moment. Or if we hadn't gotten a ride with Uncle Bruce that morning. If Mrs. Smith hadn't happened down the hall at the very same moment. If we had run left down to the lake, instead of right toward the sky tower trail—

I might still be friends with Eliza right now.

twenty-five

So yeah, we ran when we heard Mrs. Smith coming.

We weren't allowed to be eating in the lobby, or the hallway, or anywhere but the dining room, the tearoom, or outside. Technically, we weren't supposed to be inside the hotel at all. And as Eliza and I stared at the odd form of vanilla ice cream melting into the green and amber swirls of the carpet, we heard the sound of Mrs. Smith's high heels clicking on the tile floor just around the corner. So we ran.

My heart was pumping and my feet were pounding with the excitement of fear, and by the time we made it outside, far enough away from the hotel, we were laughing and we had run all the way to the base of the sky tower trail, to the hiking trail.

• • •

The last and only other time Eliza and I had taken the hiking trail to the sky tower was at the beginning of the summer, over a month ago. That time we didn't make it very far. At first the trail is easy, like a narrow dirt road. There are thick blue lines painted on the barks of the trees so you can look ahead and see where you are going. You can turn and look behind you to see where you've come from, and how to get back. We were playing Lester and Lynette when we lost the trail.

"I don't see a blue mark anywhere," Eliza said.

"Right here. We just passed one." I turned to look at the low shrubbery we had just walked through. The ground was grassy and there was no sign of a trail. I looked ahead and it looked the same.

"Where?" Eliza asked.

"I just saw it," I said but I couldn't remember how long ago that had been. Before we crossed the little creek or since?

The ground felt dry and hollow; brown leaves were thick with croppings of rock and moss jutting out. This was definitely not the trail and there were no lines of blue paint on any trees anywhere to be seen.

"Maybe we should go back a little bit until we come to the last trail marker we passed," I said.

"Which way is that?" Eliza was turning in a circle.

"Don't do that. You're confusing me. This way." I pointed.

"No, we haven't been that way. See that hairy grapevine hanging down. We didn't pass that before. And not that big log either."

Eliza was right, but it did look like a good place to sit.

"What do we do now?" I don't even know if either one of us said that out loud but I heard it in my head. And my heart started to thump.

"We've got to keep walking," Eliza said. "We can't be too far from anything or something. C'mon."

We kept moving, without talking at all. Whereas just a few minutes before we had been escaped slaves scanning the skies for the direction to freedom, now we were plain old kids at a family resort—lost.

"What were they looking for in the sky?" I asked.

"Who?"

"I don't know. Harriet Tubman? What did they see?"

"I don't know." Eliza sounded nervous.

Stars? Wind? Cloud formations? Birds flying south for winter? I had no idea—except that we didn't know how to get back, and what reason would anyone have to come looking for us until well past dinnertime?

Thinking of dinner made me hungry.

How long had we been out here? The sun was high in the sky, nearly straight above our heads. If we didn't get back in time lunch would be over, cleaned up and packed away. Then I looked over at Eliza's face and I knew we had much more to worry about. She looked like she was about to cry. We were really lost.

I am not sure how long we wandered around, looking at the floor of the woods, pine needles and leaves, and up at the trees, at which side the moss was growing on—even though neither one of us knew which direction we needed to be heading.

Down felt right. We chose the steps that took us in that direction. The sun grew hotter, our feet hurt. I wondered how long a person can just walk. And walk and walk.

"I hear someone," Eliza said. "I think."

We both stopped to listen. It was certainly footsteps, then voices.

"Hikers," I said.

"We're back on the trail."

It was a young couple, a man and a woman holding hands, both with backpacks, khaki shorts, and straw hats. We followed them back to the hotel just in time to catch the end of the buffet lunch service.

twenty-six

O h, no. Mrs. Smith almost saw us," I said. I could hardly catch my breath, from running, from laughing so hard.

"She must have seen the ice cream by now." Eliza, too, had her hands on her knees, doubled over laughing.

Starting up the hiking trail this time was more or less a nondecision. When we finally stopped running, we just kept walking, and before we knew it, we were well into the trail that led up to the sky tower where you could see four states at the same time.

"No, six," Eliza said.

"Six?"

By my calculations we had at least two hours before Michael would be done working for his dad, plenty of time to hike up to the sky tower and head back down on the easy walking trail.

We could pay attention, walk carefully. Maybe this would be the first time we'd make it all the way to the top.

"Yeah, six," Eliza answered me.

"Which ones?" Sunlight rested on the top leaves and filtered down, dappling the dirt path. It was straight up from here.

"Well, New York," Eliza said.

"We're in New York."

"So, that's one. And New Jersey."

"Maybe Pennsylvania is one. And Connecticut."

"Maybe Delaware?" Eliza tried.

"Nah."

We kept walking. It was hot and I was carrying the backpack with our sweatshirts. I worried about sweating. Maybe if I took little steps.

The trees bent their heat-weary heads like puppy dogs lolling their tongues. We were so far from anything modern, nothing to remind us of the real world. The moss on the rocks, the dirt under our feet, the blue, blue sky above our heads could be from any time, any century, any world—when Indians lived, when fairies flew, when friends held hands and made believe.

And for a little while at least, I stopped thinking about Michael, whether I was sweating, or what time it was, or Mrs. Smith, or Iraq, or even my mother. We even stopped trying to figure out the last two states.

Instead I worried the bottom of my long skirt would get caught on the brambles as the trail got steeper and narrower the closer we got to our campsite. The rest of the children would be gathering wood to get us through the coming winter. Cousin Eliza had just reminded me about how we lost little Jack during the coldest months last year. He caught a chill and just never recovered. Everyone was waiting for us to return with the mail. A package had come from the Sears & Roebuck Company.

Olden-Day Eliza could hardly contain her excitement. "I can't wait to find out what's inside," she said.

"Well, be careful. Don't shake it. It might break."

"It's too heavy to break." Eliza frowned and then, from inside my backpack my cell phone buzzed.

Or maybe it was the other way around, but either way it took me a while to register what was going on. It was the same feeling as when I am reading a really good book and I forget I am reading at all. The real world—a voice, the sound of the television—feels like an intrusion. The way you can fall in a dream and wake up in your own bed, wondering which is more real.

Michael.

It must be.

Everything fell away, the long dresses and high button boots, the package wrapped in brown paper, even the memories of little Jack and long, cold winters. The trail was narrow, and I let my step fall back behind Eliza. I was able to reach inside my back-pack and quietly take out my cell phone.

It was from Michael. I recognized the number. And there was a text message:

CAN YOU MEET ME IN GAZEBO AT THE LILY POND

I knew the lily pond. There two old pictures of it around the hotel. One in the hall to the dining room that showed a group of girls all dressed in sailor suits, all holding insect nets, with a man in a dark suit and straw hat standing behind them. The square brass plaque underneath says it is a nature expedition.

PROFESSOR ARTHUR WHITWORTH; CIRCA 1896.

And the other black-and-white photograph taken at the lily pond shows two people sitting inside the wooden summerhouse, just like the ones Uncle Bruce takes care of all year long. You can't really make out the people in the picture, but it is clearly a man and a woman with their arms wrapped around each other and their lips pressed close together. There is no plaque under-neath this photograph, which hangs, out of the way, in a far cor-ner of the tearoom behind the cherrywood and red velvet settee. You'd have to step over the furniture and then stand facing the corner to really see it, but anyone and everyone who has both-ered knows that the photograph is called "The First Kiss."

twenty-seven

We can't go back now," Eliza shouted. "We are much more than halfway to the tower."

"No way, " I tried. "We've only been hiking for a few minutes. We can go back from here. " But the truth was, I really had no idea. A hundred years had come and then gone. Lester, Lynette, photographs, and wagon trains, and generations of Villiator families, tease-y groups, and hair color camps disappeared in a second, in the single second it took for a text to buzz.

"Julia, c'mon, why do you want to quit now?"

"I'm not quitting."

I was already imagining Michael waiting at the lily pond. I needed to get there even though I was terrified at the thought. Nothing else mattered. I stopped walking and looked behind us. Down is easier. Faster.

"No, Eliza. Let's go back. It's late already. And I'm so hot."

But Eliza hadn't stopped with me. She was way ahead, determined.

"C'mon, Eliza. We can do this another time."

And that's when she stopped walking. She kept her back to me for such a long moment, I wondered what she was looking at but I was afraid to ask. I didn't want anything to distract me—or now *us*—from our task.

I had no idea how I was going to get to the lily pond alone, but I couldn't worry about that yet. One thing at a time. First, to turn around and go back to the hotel.

"You think I don't know?" Eliza's voice projected deep into the woods ahead.

"What?" I had tried to make sure Eliza hadn't seen it but maybe she heard it buzz. So I said it again with even more disbelief. "What are you talking about?"

"Julia!" Eliza shouted.

There are those times you know it's over but you act like it's not. You know you are caught but you try to ignore that for as long as possible. I watched Eliza slowly turn around and face me. Her eyes were shot with red and her lips were so tightly pressed together, white.

"Julia—" When she finally spoke again it was softly. "I know everything. I know why you wanted to go to the outdoor movie.

And all the times you made me walk by the stables. Up the mountain, down the mountain. You think I don't know why, Julia?"

I couldn't think of anything to say. Faking innocence just seemed like a waste of time, and besides, time was still moving forward. I needed to get somewhere. I needed Eliza to just start walking back with me.

"I know, Julia. And I didn't say anything. Ever. But this is different. We were having fun." Then she tried one last thing. "You can't betray a Villiator."

There wasn't anything I could say. I couldn't explain it myself. I couldn't lie anymore. But I couldn't include her either. This was about me. Michael was waiting for me. And that made me special.

It made my skin tingle and my mind full. It was like playing Lester and Lynette but it was real. Every girl needs to remember her first kiss and this could be my memory.

If I didn't go now I might miss it. Michael would never talk to me again. No boy would like me again. And if Eliza were really my friend she would understand how worried I was. She would want this for me. She would want to help me. All I had to do was explain this to her, but this is what I said instead:

"Just because a boy doesn't like you, Eliza, doesn't mean no boy should like me."

I watched her face change, from angry to hurt. Confusion and sadness. Her lips looked pressed together like a plastic mask's. I watched Eliza's body go stiff, like a doll still fastened in her box. Her clothes were fake, no real buttonholes, the material thin and held together with hidden Velcro.

Well, maybe Eliza didn't want to be real.

But I did.

twenty-eight

During World War II sixty-seven army nurses and eleven navy nurses were captured by the Japanese and held in a prisoner of war camp in the Philippines called Santo Tomas. The prison had once been a university, so maybe it wasn't so awful. But they didn't get to talk to their children or their husbands, or let anyone at home know they were okay, for three years.

More than two hundred American women serving during that war died—sixteen from enemy actions and the rest from diseases like malaria and influenza.

More numbers.

Some were even buried overseas, far from their families.

How do you know someone is really dead if you don't see their body? You might always wonder if it was a mistake. Dog tags that got mixed together. A wrong assumption.

A wrong number, after all.

They get the wrong person.

A terrible mistake.

I did. I left Eliza on the hiking trail to the sky tower. She walked one way, I walked the other. I went back, she kept going, following the blue markers. I imagined she would stay on the trail and make her way back, but the truth is, when I got nearer to the lily pond, Eliza was the last thing I was thinking about. It was as if there were a movie camera, filming me. And Michael was watching the movie.

I could picture in my mind just what I looked like walking along the grass path to the lily pond. I had given special thought to what I wore that morning (hoping I would happen to see Michael, never imagining he would want to meet me), my purple shorts and a matching halter top. I brushed my hair and pulled it into a neat ponytail. At the last minute I took it out and let it fall loose. Now I saw it bouncing across my shoulders and my back as I took deliberately slow steps for the camera. Well, maybe not bouncing, exactly. But who knows?

So how do you know if someone is about to kiss you?

What do you do?

Kiss them back or just let it happen?

Maybe I had it all wrong and Michael didn't want to kiss me at all.

I slowed down. What if he wasn't there?

Something about the idea of being the one who was waiting didn't feel right to me. I came around the corner on the grassy path and tried to see inside the wooden summer gazebo. I was pretty sure I saw a figure inside, not sitting, but standing by the corner beam. It was hard to tell in the shadows. I stepped closer before I could change my mind and back out all together. If he heard my footsteps he'd turn around and the choice would be made for me.

I let my foot rustle the dry grass and loose stones just ever so slightly.

But what if it's not him? What if someone else is in that summerhouse?

"Julia?"

The figure inside stepped out in the sunlight. It was Michael.

"Hey," I answered. Oh, lame.

"You got my text?"

I thought I had answered back, but I realized I hadn't, which meant Michael had shown up not knowing if I'd be here or not.

Or maybe he had just been here when he texted me.

In fact, maybe he had been texting someone else and sent it to me by mistake. Was that possible?

"You been here before?" Michael asked me.

"Huh?"

"Here at the pond."

"Oh, no—I mean, yes." I wasn't sure which response worked better. I didn't even know what I wanted to have work or not. "I mean, I knew where it was."

We both started walking toward the water and the path that circled the pond. Tall, fragile grasses stood up right along the edge in clumps like tufts of hair, and hundreds of lily pads floated on the surface of the water. They were all different sizes and shades of green, some with delicate stems rising from their centers. And dotting the mass of green were bursts of colorful pink and white and magenta blossoms just sitting patiently in the still heat of the day.

"Wow," I said.

"Yeah, isn't it amazing?"

I felt his hand brush against mine as we walked.

"There must be a hundred of them," Michael said as if we were just talking, as if I hadn't just moved my arm ever so slightly toward his. It was the smallest gesture and I have no idea why I thought I could do that. Or how I knew what might happen if I did.

"Probably two hundred, really. Maybe more." And he took my hand with his, letting his fingers wrap gently around mine.

I felt the stickiness of his skin, his palm—the tips of his fingers taking hold, claiming this moment.

Then just as he stopped and turned to face me, a giant white bird with his legs dangling behind him flew across the clear blue sky. Despite his size, the bird landed in the water quietly and gracefully.

Magic, I thought—as Michael leaned his face toward me and I didn't move away. The space between us got smaller and smaller until his mouth and nose, and eyes and skin were close I could hear him, feel him breathing.

This is it.

Uncountable numbers—like grains of sand, the miles from home, change in time zone, months and months of waiting. And the fear and the fear and the fear all melted away when he kissed me. And then, I think I kissed him back.

twenty-nine

I walked, I ran, I flew back to the house. I touched my lips to make sure it was real. It was. I opened the front door.

"Eliza's not back?" It was so impossible that I repeated it twice.

But it was true. It was pretty late and Eliza wasn't home yet. Only nobody looked worried. Uncle Bruce had gotten home and was already sitting in his special armchair in front of the television with a beer. Aunt Louisa was cooking dinner, chicken cutlets.

Nobody was worried until they saw me standing in the doorway, alone.

"Where is she, Julia?" Aunt Louisa asked me. She held a spatula in one hand, her other cupping the oil that might drip off the end. "Isn't she with you?"

I had a sudden image of Eliza on the hiking trail heading off in the opposite direction. Her skinny shoulders set firmly, her feet carrying her forward, up the rocky path. But we had been still very far from the sky tower. We hadn't even gotten to the Lemon Squeeze yet or crossed the Dueling Dam Bridge.

And she was alone.

Every measure of joy and excitement that had carried me all the way here drained from my face in an instant and Aunt Louisa saw it.

"What, Julia? What is it? What's wrong?"

I had never heard her sound that way and even though I was the one who knew that Eliza might be lost, Aunt Louisa's voice scared me.

My mouth opened but no words came out. I saw Uncle Bruce get up from his chair. By the time he walked into the kitchen he had his truck keys in his hand. "I'll go up to the hotel and get her, Louisa. Stay here in case Eliza gets back and I don't pass her on the way up."

"Can I go with you?" I asked Uncle Bruce.

He looked at me as if he knew there was something I was too afraid to say, as if he knew something was serious.

"Okay, let's go."

My heart was thumping by the time I slipped into the front seat of the truck. I was calculating the time that had passed. I must have left Eliza around eleven, maybe ten thirty. I met Michael at the Lily Pond around eleven fifteen, but that suddenly seemed like another life, another movie. Eliza couldn't still be on the trail. It couldn't have taken her more than an hour and half to get up there and another hour to get down even if she were walking backward!

Then even if she hung out at the hotel, maybe visited with Pam or went to the tea, she'd still be back already. Eliza hated to be alone. She wouldn't have gone swimming by herself. She wouldn't have gone to the game room or the shuffleboard court. I didn't even think she'd really go through with it and finish the hike. I guess I figured she'd just turn around like I did.

But the truth was I hadn't thought about Eliza at all. Not until right now. I could feel my fingers going a little numb as Uncle Bruce and I rode the road up to the hotel. Where could she be?

Uncle Bruce didn't say a word until we got to the fork and road changed to two-way traffic. "Tell me what happened, Julia," Uncle Bruce said quietly. "Did you two have another argument?"

I think I must have nodded. "We were on the hiking trail," I began.

I looked out the window. The end of summer was creeping across the sky and taking away the day just that much earlier than it had the night before. It would be dark in couple of hours. I knew then that Eliza was lost on the trail, and my eyes stung with tears.

"I turned around and came back," I continued. "Eliza didn't."

Uncle Bruce didn't talk at all. He kept his eyes on the road as we pulled into the staff parking lot behind the stables and he shut off the ignition. When Uncle Bruce got out of the car, I followed.

"Okay, I've got to let Mrs. Smith know. And I've got to alert the staff."

"You do?"

I had an image of how angry Mrs. Smith would be. I could just see her face.

"And the night manager. He'll have the two-way radios."

"What?" I asked, but Uncle Bruce was already heading into the hotel. I had to break into a run to keep just behind him and near enough. He didn't answer me. It was as if every step he took he got more and more anxious. I could feel it, like a string tightening around my stomach, a string that became a rope that became a heavy chain. I could hardly breathe. I was so afraid for Eliza.

And just underneath the tightening in my chest I was afraid for myself.

"Exactly where, what part of the trail did you last see her?"

the night manager was asking me. "Be very specific. This is important."

The night manager was a tall man, because when he stood up from behind his desk I had to look way up at him. He had a very serious expression on his face, that kind of grown-up way of acting like everything was going to be all right when, in fact, he was very worried.

I pointed on the map as close as I could remember to where we were standing when Eliza and I had our fight. And I left her there.

"And do you remember what time it was?" he said. "As close to exactly as you can."

I knew. I took out my phone and looked at the time of Michael's text. "Ten thirty-three."

Uncle Bruce looked stricken but he didn't say anything to me. "Does that help, Steve?" Uncle Bruce asked. The night manager's name was Steve.

"Well, we can do an approximation," Steve said, taking some maps out of a drawer and spreading them out on the desktop, "of what the average person on foot can cover in say, an hour or two. Even at a leisurely pace a healthy person could travel three to four miles without even knowing it. We've had hikers end up over in Accord."

"You mean Eliza could have walked right out of Mohawk?

Not be in New Hope any more?" I heard myself cry out and then I felt Uncle Bruce's hand on my shoulder. It was comforting and warning.

"No need to panic, sweetie. We are going to find her. She might even be right here in the hotel. It happens." Steve spoke slowly and directly to me. "So you are going to have to tell us—"

"Julia," Uncle Bruce filled in.

"And be honest, Julia. Is there any reason Eliza might be upset? Is there any reason she might not want to be found?"

"Maybe," I answered.

thirty

uge halogen lights that were normally used to dry
paint on the walls in large rooms were set up on
the roof of the hotel and lit up the sky like strange white suns.
They were supposed to act as directional beacons in case Eliza
was out there somewhere, nearby, and might follow them back
to the hotel.

Every available staff member who knew the trails had been
sent out with a two-way radio. The recreation staff, the activity
staff, and even the maintenance staff, like Uncle Bruce, everyone took a different trail and followed it from start to end. The
rest of the staff searched inside the hotel, checking first all the
places they thought a kid might be—the game room, the television room, and of course the gift shop.

"No, no, I haven't seen Eliza all day. But she's always with

Julia. Have you asked Julia? I haven't seen either of them all day. They must be together. Are you sure she went up to the sky tower?"

Pam didn't see me standing behind Uncle Bruce. "Oh my, it's so dark out now." Her face was so filled with concern it made my stomach twist even more. Then Pam spotted me lingering near the rock-candy sticks. "Julia, thank goodness. Where's Eliza?" she asked me. She still didn't get it.

But a second later she did.

"Eliza is lost, isn't she? How long?"

She was asking me but the night manager answered. "It's been several hours already, Pam. You know what to do if she shows up here. Or if you hear anything."

"Of course, Steve," Pam said. When she turned to look at the approaching darkness outside I wondered what she was thinking about. Maybe she was remembering that little girl who two years ago wandered away from her family to get a sweater that she had left on a picnic bench and didn't return. The mother was certain she had been snatched and she was hysterical for hours, until a doctor was called to give her a sedative. A kid doesn't get lost walking fifty yards to the picnic lodge, the mother kept screaming until the medicine finally kicked in and she fell asleep on a chair in the grand sitting room.

But it turns out they can. And by the time the mother woke

up, her little girl was back in her arms. She had just taken a wrong turn. The little girl had her sweater but had somehow lost her right sneaker. Eliza told me all about it in school the next day.

Or maybe Pam was remembering the boy who had walked back into the hotel after his parents had checked out and his whole family was in their car ready to drive away. The boy said he left his iPod on the little glass table right beside the checkout counter. He ran back inside to get it, but he never came back out. That boy was found about an hour later walking down the mountain road toward the gatehouse with his headset on. He explained to everyone he decided to leave out the front door and that his parents would drive by and see him on their way home.

"He really thought his parents would just leave without him," Eliza had told me. "Isn't that crazy?"

Then it was completely dark, eight o'clock, and as is the procedure, Mrs. Smith called the state troopers, who arrived with their dogs.

thirty-one

The officer wanted something of Eliza's so his people-sniffing dogs could pick up her scent and begin to track her. Uncle Bruce called Aunt Louisa, who he still insisted wait at the house in case Eliza showed up there. Two neighbors had come over, made coffee, and offered to stay with her. One of them could drive something of Eliza's up to the hotel. A pair of socks, a nightgown would be great, the officer told us. Anything that hadn't been laundered.

"Will this work?" I asked. I fished into my backpack and brought out Eliza's sweatshirt.

"Does this belong to the missing girl?" the officer asked me.

I nodded. But Eliza is not a missing girl.

"Did she wear it today?"

"Yes," I answered. "She always wears that one. It hasn't been washed all summer."

Eliza's sweatshirt was pink with a hood and a zipper. It looked suddenly so small and so pink when the police officer took it from me. His uniform was gray, and his belt was black and he had a gun.

We were in the grand tearoom that had been closed off so that the sight of the state troopers and the dogs, and the lights, the megaphones, the maps, and the walkie-talkies that gave off periodic random static wouldn't affect the other guests. It was clear that people knew something was going on, but so far no one had said anything. Mrs. Smith was standing by the tea tray holding her own hands tightly, as tightly as her face was pinched into an angry, worried expression.

Steve, the night manager, was by the glass doors talking quietly with two staffers, a youngish guy and an older woman. I recognized them as trail guides.

Uncle Bruce was poring over the open maps and I noticed for the first time the tiny shapes of flowers and vines carved into the legs of the wooden table where he was standing. Not saying a word, like he was trying to remember something. Where was that steep drop? That crevasse that someone could fall into? Where was that one spot where the trail narrows and the colored markers are most faded?

The Korean War is called the Forgotten War because nobody seems to care about it. It happened right after the end of World War II and before the Vietnam War. When the Korean War veterans came home from their tour of duty, there were no memorials or parades, not much on the evening news, not even any protests or demonstrations. It wasn't even called a war. It was called a conflict. The Korean conflict.

But if you ask me no one cares about any war.

If it doesn't affect them personally, they can act like it isn't happening. If it isn't in their backyard or even within a thousand miles it might as well be a cartoon on TV or a boring reality show. If their mom or dad isn't over there eating sand, it hardly matters. No, it doesn't matter at all. How can you forget about something you never knew about in the first place?

Fifty thousand women were on active duty in Korea and even though women were not allowed in direct combat and still are not, army nurse Genevieve Smith died in a plane crash on her way to Korea. One navy nurse died when her hospital ship was rammed by a freighter, right off the coast of California. Eleven nurses died in a plane crash on the way to Japan. Vera Brown died in a plane crash and so did two other air force nurses. And maybe back home, their own kid was just eating dinner when it happened. Maybe right at the moment their mom or dad got killed they were biting into a hot dog. Or pitching the ball in a kickball game. Brushing their hair. Staring at a pimple in the mirror and getting really upset about it.

You can't ever let down your guard. You can't ever stop remembering and paying attention or anything could happen. And then it really started to sink in.

This was my fault.

All of it.

Eliza heading off on the trail. The state troopers being here. The dogs burying their snouts in Eliza's pink sweatshirt and getting all excited, wagging their tails and turning circles on the colorful carpet in the grand tearoom. Mrs. Smith wringing her hands. Aunt Louisa pacing back and forth in the kitchen, looking out her window at the night pressing in, maybe even crying like I imagined she would be.

—The halogens on the roof lighting up the sky.

—Now the dogs barking and pulling on their leashes. (Dogs aren't even allowed at Mohawk.)

—Everyone out on the trails with flashlights and walkie-talkies shouting out into the darkness. "Eliza! Eliza! Can you hear me?"

All of this for a boy.

All this for one kiss.

thirty-two

Even though nobody knew the trails better than Uncle Bruce, he was told to stay put.

"It happens every time." The trooper held his wide felt hat in his hands and rubbed the brim with his fingers as he spoke to us. "We find the lost person and then we have to send everyone back out to find the family members who went out looking on their own. We call it double indemnity."

We were sitting together on couches—me, Uncle Bruce, Steve, Pam, and Mrs. Smith—waiting, but I couldn't get my heart to settle down, not for one second. I tried holding my breath so that I would take in less oxygen, but I just felt light-headed. I tried visualizing a calming waterfall, like I heard about on one of Aunt Louisa's talk shows, but I kept thinking of Eliza splashing around crying for help.

When my phone vibrated it took me a full second to realize what it was. It was another text from Michael.

I think I know where Eliza might be.

My heart went wild. I looked around the room as if anyone else could have heard it. I typed back.

What are you talking about? How could you know?

My cell phone buzzed back immediately.

Don't tell anyone. Meet me behind the stables. ASAP.

I flipped my phone shut and stood up. "I'm just going to the restroom." I said out loud, but no one was paying attention to me anyway. After I had explained exactly where I last saw Eliza, there wasn't anything anyone wanted from me.

"Just don't go anywhere," the state trooper told me.

I guess he was trained to notice things. I wonder if he suspected anything, if he knew it was all my fault. I nodded and as soon as I was out of eyeshot, I darted toward the back porch and down the steps. I took them two at a time, landed on the gravel with a thud, and took off running straight into the darkness.

"Julia?"

"Where are you?" I whispered back. I couldn't see anything. The smell of animals and hay and manure was strong in the night air. I could hear the horses snorting and shifting around in their stalls.

"Right here." Michael's hand just barely brushed the back of my shirt, but I jumped. "It's just me."

"I know," I said. Finally I could see him in the shadows, but clearly. We were alone together again. It was only a few hours ago he kissed me but it felt like a hundred years. What had been the most important moment of my life was barely a memory anymore. The knot in my stomach had swallowed it right up, but if we could find Eliza maybe I could make this all better.

Maybe.

"So why do you think you know?" I asked Michael. "What could you possibly know?"

"I know all the hiding places," Michael told me.

I knew Michael's dad was one of the staff, like Uncle Bruce, but Michael's family had housing right here on Mohawk grounds. It did make sense he would know something like that.

"Okay, so why don't we just tell someone?"

There was one bare bulb at the end of the barn near the wide doors. We headed toward it. "I thought maybe I could be a hero," Michael said.

Being a hero sure sounded better than being the bad guy.

"And me?" I asked.

"Yeah, sure."

Everybody loves a hero.

thirty-three

Everybody loved Jessica Lynch. She was a private in the regular army. She got a Bronze Star, which is for "heroic or meritorious achievement or service," and she got a Purple Heart, which is a medal for getting wounded (or killed) by the enemy.

She was part of a convoy of the 507th army maintenance unit that was ambushed by Iraqi forces. The Humvee she was traveling in turned over, and Jessica was badly injured but she lived and she was taken prisoner.

That was in 2003 and my mom hadn't been deployed yet, but we all knew it was coming. We just didn't talk about it. She had been in the National Guard for two years; already some of the other nurses she trained with at "summer camp" were in Iraq. A lot had been sent to Afghanistan. We just never talked about it.

The story of Jessica Lynch was all over the news that spring. They even had footage of the Army Special Forces breaking into the Baghdad hospital where she was prisoner, and taking her out on a stretcher. She had both legs in casts and a big bandage around her head. She looked scared. She was nineteen years old. My mom and dad and I didn't want to watch but we couldn't help it. Everyone was talking about it. Wondering what had happened to her. Was she tortured—or worse—because she was a woman?

Then we saw the video of Shoshana Johnson, who was also captured the same day, in the same attack, but she didn't get rescued for another twelve days. On the TV, one of her captors was holding a microphone right in front of her face and demanding answers. Shoshana looked terrified, her eyes darting left and right. Her terrible fear was so clear, so real.

It was like watching a really scary horror movie. Your brain had to remind you that this was not acting. This was a woman. Somebody's mother.

"She's just the army cook," my mother told us.

We were in the living room watching the news. The dishwasher was turned on and humming in the kitchen. It had been my favorite time of the day. We are all content and stuffed from dinner. There is not enough time to start anything too big or too busy but it's too early to get ready for bed. My mom's usually too tired to start bugging me about my homework. My dad doesn't watch much TV, so he just flips through the channels. Usually he puts on the news. That's when we saw Shoshana Johnson.

"How do you know?" my dad asked.

"One of the nurses at the hospital. She's in the Guard too. And she's from Texas. Like her, like Shoshana. She told us at lunch today. It's just terrible."

On the screen they flashed photos of Shoshana from her childhood. They had some guy who had been a POW during the Vietnam War reliving his experiences. They talked about the seven other soldiers still being held and what their captivity might be like but nobody really knew. They talked about Lori Ann Piestewa whose body was found when they rescued Jessica Lynch. Lori Ann Piestewa was the first Native American woman killed in military service. So for a while everybody acted like they cared. Or pretended they did.

But what I will always remember is that Lori Ann Piestewa was the first American woman to die in Iraq.

thirty-four

Michael and I moved as close as we could along the huge stone foundation on the far end of the hotel, behind the prickly shrubs and tall, thick hydrangea bushes so no one would see us. Every few minutes another staffer or two would walk by, a beam of light tracking back and forth across the walkway in front, calling out.

One kid we recognized as a busboy from the kitchen staff was singing hip-hop lyrics and clicking his flashlight on and off like a strobe. He clearly wasn't too worried about finding Eliza.

"Where are we going?" I asked Michael when the rapper had passed and seemed far enough away.

"Just stay close. And quiet."

There was something about being told what to do by a boy that I liked and at the same time made me completely annoyed. And I wasn't sure which would make me look better to Michael, saying something cute and angry? Or just doing what I was told?

Honestly, what did I care what Michael-what's-his-name thinks of me?

I heard one of the ladies in the tearoom asking Mrs. Smith if she thought Eliza had been abducted. Certainly not, Mrs. Smith had said. My stomach lurched again thinking of that.

"Just a little farther." Michael didn't turn around but I saw his hand, his fingers reach out behind him. I took his hand. It was rough and warm and we broke into a run across the great lawn and into the night.

"Eliza, we know you are up there."

"She is?"

I saw Michael shrug his shoulders at me as if to say, *I don't know but it's worth a try.* Then he lifted his head and looked back up into the tree.

"Eliza, come down from the tree," he said.

It was not an ordinary tree and if Eliza were here, I couldn't believe that she had climbed up into these branches. I couldn't believe that she had never taken me here before. Michael had called it the elephant tree and now I could see why.

The trunk of this tree was thick and wrinkled, like the skin of an elephant. The branches were low and tangled. They hung like hundreds of elephant trunks, dangling close to the ground and reaching upward into an intricate mass of steps and swings and balconies. In contrast to the massive form of bark and trunk and branches, its leaves were tiny and delicate, almost like little feathers. It was a tree meant to be climbed. To hide away in.

And then like magic Eliza's voice came down from the tippy top. "What do you two want?"

"Eliza! Is that you? It's you!" I picked up my head and shouted. My relief was indescribable. She was found and she was safe. I could tell by her voice, Eliza was all right. The weight lifted off my chest.

It took me only a few moments more to get mad.

"Eliza, everyone is looking for you. Don't you know that? Don't you know how late it is?"

Of course she did. It was way past dark, pitch-black in fact, and besides, Eliza had to see those lights on the roof of the hotel. She probably heard the dogs barking. She must have heard everyone calling out her name.

And she still hadn't come down from the tree.

She let everybody worry about her. She had to know what big trouble I was going to be in. Maybe that was her plan all along.

"We saved you," Michael spoke up. "Now come down."

Eliza's little voice shot back. "No."

Eliza hadn't ever been lost; she was hiding, but Michael still seemed bent on being a hero.

"Well, you are going to come down and walk back with us or I'm going to start shouting," he threatened. "And I bet Mrs. Smith comes over."

I looked at him. "Are you going to pretend you just found her?"

"Well, it would look better for all of us, wouldn't it?" he answered.

I could hear rustling in the branches and leaves above, like Eliza was shifting around. Maybe ready to come down. Maybe not.

"I got scared." Eliza's voice was closer but I still couldn't see her.

"Of what?" I asked.

"I never went up to the sky tower. I just waited until you were far enough away and then I went back."

It was the first time I got to rewind the images in my head. Eliza was never lost in the woods, lying with a twisted ankle or fallen in some deep ravine. I could breathe. "So where were you this whole time?" Michael asked.

"I just waited. I waited in one of the gazebos. I think I fell asleep. I thought you'd come back, Julia. I thought you couldn't have just left me there. But you did."

I listened.

"Then it was starting to get dark," she went on. "And I decided to make you worried. I just wanted to see if you'd get worried and come back for me. I never thought everyone would start looking for me."

I could hear the tears coming into Eliza's voice.

She was crying. "I didn't know what to do. So I came here."

"To the elephant tree," Michael filled in.

"Yeah. We used to hide here when we were kids. We had a clubhouse for a while."

"Who's 'we'?" I asked because I knew it wasn't me. I didn't even know about this hiding place. And I couldn't believe Eliza had friends I didn't know about.

"Me, Michael, and those kids whose parents both worked here and then they moved away. Remember them, Michael? We all used to come here."

I guess you don't really know someone until you almost lose them.

I could see Eliza's foot and then one of her bare legs. She was still in shorts. She must have been freezing.

"When I saw the police cars coming, then I got really scared. I had no idea so much time had gone by," Eliza said.

"C'mon," I said. "We have to go back or else they are going to start looking for all of us."

She dropped to the ground. "Okay, but I'm still really mad at you."

"Well, I'm still mad at you," I said.

"Well, we're not going to tell them the truth, are we?" Michael complained.

I still wasn't sure what the truth really was, but somehow I still had the feeling that once Eliza was found safe, the focus was going to turn to me. The state troopers. Aunt Louisa. Uncle Bruce. Even Mrs. Smith knew I was the last one with Eliza, so even if she wasn't lost I was still the one who walked away and left her.

And after everyone stopped being worried about Eliza they were going to get real mad. At me.

And boy, was I right.

thirty-five

There was another joke going around last spring. It went like this:

What's the five-day forecast for Baghdad?

Answer: Two days.

I didn't hear that one from Peter, though. I heard it on TV, on a stand-up comedy show, and I was the one who came to school and told it to him.

"That's not funny," Peter said.

Mrs. Jaffe had just walked out of the room for a minute. We were supposed to be writing in our journals.

"You just don't get it," I said.

"I get it. It's just not funny."

I guess I knew that already. The five-day forecast? Like

a weather report, only no one in Baghdad is going to live long enough for it to matter. That's not funny. I felt terrible.

When Michael, Eliza, and I got back to the hotel, we walked straight into the tearoom, which had become some kind of a operations headquarters, and we stood waiting for someone to notice us.

I don't know how long we actually stood there, but it was Uncle Bruce who finally shouted out, "Eliza!"

And then it got real quiet. For a long moment all you could hear was the empty static of the two-way radios—until one of the dogs resting on the floor lifted his nose into the air and took a giant sniff. The dog jumped up and started barking, followed by the other two, then all of them came running toward us. The dogs went crazy circling around Eliza, whining and howling, trying with everything they had not to jump right on top of her.

I can hardly remember anything after that.

Except the barrage of questions.

And Eliza crying.

She started crying so hard that no one was ever going to be mad at her. She cried so hard her face got puffy and red and her voice was warbly with mucus. I could only make out a couple of words, like "sorry" and "scared" and that was enough. At almost the same time Michael was talking, really fast like he was trying to outrun the wrong question.

"Remember? That's when the Miller twins lived up here too. Remember their dad was an electrician and their mom was a sous-chef? We all used to play together. We made a club in this tree—"

I don't know who he was talking to really, but he was on a roll. Eliza was down to an involuntary but loud, sniffling inhale of breath that made everyone turn to look at her.

"Then I remember that guest's kid—remember? Last fall or something," Michael went on. "When we all thought she was lost but it turned out she was hiding under the bed. The cleaning crew didn't even see her—remember? Remember that? So that's when I thought—"

He would have kept going and going, trying to make everyone think he was a hero, forgetting all about including me, but Mrs. Smith put up her hand and stopped him. She stopped everyone, even the dogs.

"It's over," she said. "Everyone back to work."

I think my problem was I didn't cry.

My mother was supposed to be coming home soon. Summer was just about over. I started seventh grade in two weeks. It all worked out, any way you cut it.

Except that my dad took away my cell phone, forever.

Eliza hadn't said two words to me since she got grounded for her part in the whole mess.

Mrs. Smith said she was going to reevaluate the privileges of the workers' children on the grounds.

And I hadn't seen Michael since the day he kissed me, and the night we all got in big trouble.

But other than that everything was just perfect.

"A friend is someone who knows the song in your heart, and can sing it back to you when you have forgotten the words."

—*Unknown*

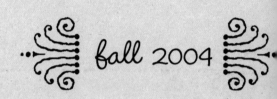

fall 2004

My dad and I are going into town to buy school supplies. I wanted to wait until my mom got back but my dad said he had the money and there were big sales at Walmart. So we are going. But it's not the same.

Besides, my dad told me, when my mom comes home she may not really want to run out and battle the crowds at Walmart. I thought that was a funny choice of words.

My dad doesn't like to push the shopping cart. He says it makes him feel silly, so I have two fists on the handle and we are heading into the store. The cart is huge and there's a big yellowy smiley face staring at me from the plastic seat. There are people everywhere, all gripping other huge metal carts with big yellow smiley faces and racing around the store. There is old-people music coming out of the ceiling speakers. Someone dropped a jar of grape jelly on the floor and I just barely miss stepping in it.

I look at my dad and he has that let's-hurry-up expression, right along with the how-much-is-this-going-to-cost? look on his face.

So my summer is over, but it's like it never happened. There's the aftermath of an explosion, you can't remember much, and all you know is nothing is going to be the same. Last year when I had gone school shopping, my mom took me. We already knew she was leaving for Iraq. I wasn't sure if I wanted everything in the store or nothing at all—I just knew I didn't want my mother to leave.

"Let me see that list again, Julia," my mother said. She held out her hand.

"You have it."

"No, I don't," she answered. She stopped moving the cart down the aisle and planted her feet. "I gave it back to you."

This was right at the peak of our pre-deployment fighting. All of us, especially me and my mom. But I was certain she had my school supply list. It had come in the mail along with my teacher assignments. It was my first year that I'd be changing classrooms. A different teacher for math, one for language arts, another for science, and a whole period of Spanish. And each teacher sent a list of things they wanted us to have for the first day of sixth grade.

I was worried about finding each classroom. I was worried about being late. I was worried about who would help me with my homework. Who would make my lunch every day?

But I was certain my mother put the list in her pocketbook before we left for Walmart.

"It's in your bag, Mom." We were blocking half the boys' underwear section and a traffic jam was developing all the way to socks and pajamas.

"Julia, I know I gave it to you just before we got out of the car. I can't keep track of everything. Did you lose it?"

"Not everything is my fault, Mom." I could hear my voice rising and my lips were beginning to quiver. I started to get that burning feeling deep in my chin like a little electric pulse that seems to activate the crying mechanism. After that there's no turning back. I didn't want to cry. The more you fight it the more your chin stings with electricity.

"Excuse me, ladies, would you mind handing me that package of the blue boxer briefs, extra large?" The man who had come up behind us pointed.

I don't even remember if we ever found the list of supplies, and if we did, which one of us had it, but I remember we both started laughing. We walked up and down every aisle and bought everything I could possibly need, pens, mechanical pencils, notebooks, folders. In every color. And even though I had mine from last year, my mom picked out a brand-new backpack for me.

"No, I don't need one, Dad," I say.

"You sure? They look nice."

I shake my head and my dad puts the backpack back on its hook. I know he is trying. A voice comes over the speakers and tells us there will be a markdown in housewares on all coffeemakers and dehumidifiers and suddenly, for no reason related to either of those two things, I can't wait for my mom to come home. After all these months and months, all through sixth grade and the whole summer I was okay. I worried and I missed my mom but I was okay—and now it's like I can't stand it another minute.

I am going to burst.

I want my mother, right here. Right now. In Walmart.

"I want to go look at the auto section for a second. You okay here, alone?" my dad asks me. "I just want to see if they have one thing. You get what you need, okay?"

"Sure, Dad. I'll meet you at the checkout."

And it is like my dad is feeling the same exact thing I am. He leans over and kisses my forehead. "She'll be home soon. We did it, Julia. We did it and she'll be home soon."

This time I nod and take a deep breath.

"I'm fine, Dad." And I am.

I don't see Peter Vos right away. First I hear him.

thirty-seven

I t is coming from a couple of aisles over but it's loud enough for me to make out all the words.

And to recognize who it is.

"Dad, Dad. Calm down."

"I will calm down when I damn well want to calm down, Peter. This is completely ridiculous. There is no order to this. This is ridiculous. Doesn't anybody work around here?"

"Dad, shhh. Lower your voice, will ya?" I can hear everything in Peter's voice, everything no one understands, everything jokes can't hide. "I'll get someone," he says.

"No, this is not right. This is not how it should be."

Then I hear more shouting, a thump, and a big crash, like cardboard boxes tumbling to the floor but still something tells me to stay put. I know Peter doesn't want to see me right now. He doesn't want me to see him.

"Oh my god, Peter. I'm so sorry." It's his dad's voice, softer but panicked. I still think I should freeze and not make a sound. "Are you all right, son? Oh my god—I am so sorry."

I shouldn't be here but I don't know which way to turn. I can't tell where the sounds are coming from, down the aisle or up. If I go one way, maybe I should have gone the other. When I hear footsteps coming nearer, I pretend really hard that I am looking at something on the shelf.

And then Peter is standing there and I turn—I don't want to, but I do—and see Peter looking right at me. He knows I have heard everything.

"I hate you," he says to me. "I hate you." And he runs away.

thirty-eight

I f I think about it, my summer before boys was ending a long time before I met Michael. It wasn't even one event, like leaving Eliza on that trail. It was more like a slow process. I can't play D'Ville the way I used to. I can set up the dolls and make them go to college and make them drive in their cars, but I can't see all the details anymore. Their lips don't move. Their hair comes out of holes in their scalps. It had been that way for a while, hadn't it?

The summer before this last one, I didn't live up at Mohawk the whole time, of course, but we visited a lot. It was just about this time a year ago, just before school began, that we all went up to the hotel for Eliza's birthday.

And if I think also about that day, it was the last day of real magic. For both of us. The last time we went away completely, until we had to come in for supper. We were best friends. We were Indian captives. We were pioneers. We were Lester and Lynette.

The weather was already changing. It was hot, but the sun was lower in the sky and so it was not so *hot* hot. There was already a dryness in the air that made the leaves sound different when the wind blew. You could tell it was fall. There was a feeling of something ending and something new about to begin. There was stillness in the air like the crossover between two times, between past and present, the real and the unreal.

"If we die today," Lynette began. "If this is our last day on this earth I want you to know you are my best friend."

"We are not going to die today, Lynette," Lester told her. He was trying to be the brave one. *Boys do that,* I thought. *Boys are supposed to be unafraid.*

"But if we do—" We had stopped to make camp on the side of this mountain, beside the great lake that the Native Americans had called Mirror Water (Eliza made that up), to rest on our way back to their camp. Our fate was unknown. We both knew of stories of settlers who had been captured and never heard from again.

Lynette went on. " I just want you to know I love you."

Lester turned to Lynette. Her blonde hair fell in wisps from her sunbonnet and her young eyes filled with tears. Their shoes were worn from days of walking. Their bellies were empty from lack of food.

It would be hard to say whether Lester and Lynette were brother and sister, or girlfriend and boyfriend. Were they children or teenagers or grown-ups? Cousins or even uncle and niece? It didn't matter at all because in that moment, in that space out of time, there was no one and nothing else. They would walk on the trails to the Native American longhouse village and be adopted by a loving family who had just lost their own two babies to a terrible disease the white man had brought to this new land, and for which the tribe had no immunity. Lester and Lynette would grow up with new names. Maybe Spirit of Running Bear. Or Girl with Hair Like Corn Silk.

"Or Jumps Like Grasshopper," I said. I loved to jump.

"Sings Like Soaring Sparrow." Eliza wanted to be a famous singer when she grew up.

"Or Swims in Rushing Waters."

Eliza stopped me there. "You hate to swim."

"I do?"

I didn't like to swim and Eliza knew me.

"How about Wades in Rushing Waters, then?"

"Nice."

We could hear Aunt Louisa calling us to eat. My mom had set up the food on the outdoor table. Eliza's birthday. She was twelve. We had all her favorites: stuffed shells, fresh rolls, salad, and not cake or cupcakes but brownies. Eliza loved double chocolate brownies. And lemonade. I've always loved the taste of the sour liquid and the sweet mushy chocolate together in my mouth. I love pretzels and soda. I love apples and peanut butter.

And so does Eliza.

We sat at the table, waiting. Me and Eliza. *Eliza and I*, my mother would correct me. The cloth was laid down. The bowls were set out. The brownies were covered in tinfoil but I could still make out what they were because of the candles poking up. Uncle Bruce and my dad were standing next to each other, but not saying much. My mom and Aunt Louisa were dying laughing. I tried, but we couldn't hear what was going on.

How much harder it was that day, to pretend.

We will be packing the wagon soon anyway, Eliza said, as if I could see her long skirt and apron, her high buttoned shoes and wool stockings peeking out from her petticoat. But at the same time, I could still see Aunt Louisa and my mom and I wondered what was so funny—I wanted to know so badly. I could hear Eliza talking about wagon trains and maize but I couldn't *see* it.

I wanted to play, but it was harder to make happen.

The world hadn't yet changed one bit. The same light grew from dark blue to purplish to gray, the same ground made the same gravelly noise under our feet. I imagine the same exact stars dropped one by one into the black sky. But I was changing. Looking back, that day, what was real and what was not real was slowly starting to separate.

Like a cocoon, splitting right down the center and revealing what's inside.

Like a whistle piercing the quiet night.

Like a parent who leaves one way and comes back another, changed forever.

thirty-nine

My dad said Mom will be home by the end of the week. We got an e-mail from the United States Government. Sometimes they just change things in the army and a plane comes in early or a week late. Or not at all. So we were told to be prepared for a change of plans.

Which meant my mother could be coming home right now, flying over my head, landing on the runway.

Or she could be redeployed and have to spend another nine months, or ten months, or another full year, and there was nothing we could do about it.

Or she could take a taxi from the airfield and show up in the hallway of the middle school right now. She might see me coming out of my first day of class, and I might see her in her army fatigues and combat boots, but her hat is in her hand, and she doesn't even recognize me.

What if I've changed so much my mother doesn't know who I am?

What if my own mother doesn't recognize me?

"Julia, are you all right?"

It's my new teacher, Mr. Henry, and when I look up everyone else has piled out of homeroom and into the hall.

"Oh, yeah, sure. I was just getting all my stuff together." But I glance down and I have only a pencil to gather from my desk. Oh, brother. I think I need to shake the thoughts from yesterday out of my head.

"I'm sorry, Julia," Aunt Louisa told me over the phone, the night before our first day of school. "She just needs a little time, sweetie. You guys were so close, too close—maybe you need to give it a little space."

I don't understand.

There is no such thing as too close. Best friends cannot be too close. We didn't even talk about what we are going to wear the first day of school. What if we are wearing the same thing? What if we're not?

Last year we made a plan to wear the exact same thing, just

complete opposite. I wore jeans, a red shirt, and a white sweater and Eliza had on a white shirt, a red sweater, and jeans. Nobody noticed but every time we passed each other in the hall we laughed and said, "Nice outfit."

Today, I don't even care what I am wearing. I hope I don't even see Eliza all day.

But it's not that easy to avoid someone in New Hope Middle School. The seventh grade takes up only one hall, the upper ramp of the new part of the building. You'd almost have to poke your head out of the classroom to make sure the person you were trying to avoid wasn't in the hall, and then dart really fast to your next class. Assuming you knew exactly where that was.

Even then, there's the cafeteria.

Maybe because Eliza and I were our own group of two, I am not sure where to sit. And because my dad sent me to school this morning, I only have enough money for a sandwich and milk. So no tray. Still I feel ridiculous standing here.

I feel lost without Eliza.

I am beginning to wonder if she even came to school this morning. Then I see Eliza sitting at a table with Sophie Cutler and Tamara Williams, our mirror couple. According to the story, Sophie and Tamara got into a big fight in kindergarten over whose turn it was at the easel and when it was over, red paint and all, they were best friends. They are wearing the same outfit today, matching jean vests, white shirt, and jeans. I wonder if they have a whole village of dolls, or Legos, or Playmobile, or Beanie Babies.

Eliza is chatting with them like they've been in our group forever. Or like she's in theirs. Has she told them about the tease-y group? The hair color camp?

If I take two steps backward and a little to the right, Eliza won't see me at all. So this is exactly what I do. Of course, it means I won't get to eat lunch today but suddenly I am not sure what to do. I don't know if Eliza will ask me to sit with her or look right at me and keep talking to Sophie and Tamara like she doesn't know me at all. And I'd rather not find that out.

By the time school ends and the buses are lining up, my stomach is growling so loudly I have to pretend to cough so the kid next to me in eighth period math stops looking over at me and making faces.

Eliza takes one of the little buses that leaves from the front of the school. There are only a couple of kids that live that far up the mountain, so I know there is no chance of seeing her at the back bus loop. But I don't expect to see Peter either and here he is.

"Julia, wait up," he says. He rushes across the pavement so I have to stop.

"What?"

Peter starts breathing really hard like he's just run the mile, but I think it's more like he's buying time to figure out what to say. He puts his hand on his knee and bends over a little. I can tell he's just faking it. Then he finally lifts his head.

"I'm sorry about Walmart, you know. I didn't mean what I said."

"I know."

"I don't hate you."

"Thanks." I actually feel better hearing it.

"Wanna go to one of my soccer games?" Peter asks me.

"When?"

"After school."

"Today?" *Well, that explains the shorts and funny socks.* "Maybe another time," I say. "There's something I've got to take care of today."

"There's another one next week too, if you want to come to that one," Peter says and he hurries off.

I think he likes me.

y dad says he'll drive me up to Eliza's. He always tries to be home when I get home from school, or close to it. Today we get home about the same time.

Sure, he says when I ask him.

"Hi, Dad." Aunt Louisa's door is wide open but she gets up when she hears us. "What are you guys doing up here?"

"Julia wants to apologize to Eliza," my dad tells her.

"And you drove her all the way up here, Dad? That's real nice of you," Aunt Louisa says to Dad but she winks at me. "They're at the hotel, sweetie."

Uncle Bruce had to check on one of the gazebos. Loose railing post, Aunt Louisa told us. He needed some special tool or some such thing and he went back up with it. Eliza went with him since it was such a beautiful afternoon.

"I bet you can find them, though. Eliza will probably be hanging out with Pam at the gift shop. Go on. In fact, I'll go with you."

Aunt Louisa reaches for her sweater by the door and steps outside without waiting for an answer. We all get into my dad's car and head up to the hotel. I have to sit in the back, but I don't mind.

I listen to my dad telling Aunt Louisa that my mom is due to come home any day now. Or rather, any day now we will be getting word of her exact arrival date. I wonder if grown-ups really think you can't hear them when they lower their voices.

He is talking about what's going on in the war.

The trees are rushing past my window, too fast.

He's talking about what he heard on the news this morning. I can make out every other word or so.

The shrubs. Hills of grass. Even the pavement is eaten up under the car in a matter of seconds.

In Vietnam eight military women died, not from the flu or in a plane crash, but were killed. Like all the hundreds and hundreds of thousands of men in war before them. A lot of people were against the war in Vietnam. There were demonstrations all over the country. People who were against the war put bumper stickers on their cars showing how they felt.

MAKE LOVE NOT WAR.

And then other people put stickers on their cars that said, AMERICA: LOVE IT OR LEAVE IT.

Vietnam is called the Unpopular War, which has got to be the strangest expression ever. Can there really be such a thing as a popular war?

Eliza is in the gift shop. She is sitting on Pam's stool behind the counter. I can see her through the glass window in the hall but she can't see me. Or at least not unless she looks up. She seems to be counting something. I can see Pam helping a customer pick out a postcard from the rack.

"I can tell you one thing." I feel Mrs. Smith behind me, before I can register her voice. She even puts her hand on my shoulder. "There will be plenty of boys, Julia. Plenty of boys." And she heads off down the hall before I can figure out what she means by that.

"Julia!"

Then Eliza is standing in the hall next to me. We don't even say a word. We don't wait another minute. We just wrap our arms around each other.

"Eliza, I am so sorry," I say. "You are my best friend. I missed you so much."

"I'm sorry too, Julia."

All of a sudden I am flooded with all the things I want to tell her.

About school, my teachers. I want to ask her about Tamara and Sophie.

Hey, since when are you friends with Tamara and Sophie?

I have to tell her about my mother coming home.

I'm scared my mother will come home like Peter's dad.

About the party my dad and I are planning to have.

I'm afraid I've changed so much my mother won't recognize me.

How can we have a party for my mom's homecoming without Eliza? We can't—and now we don't have to.

"You girls look like you could use an ice cream," Pam is saying. I see she is waving at us from inside the gift shop.

I reach inside the freezer and take out an ice-cream sandwich. I take out two and I hand one to Eliza.

"Thanks," she says.

"This one's on me." Pam smiles.

forty-one

My mother will come home from Iraq. It will be a Tuesday afternoon. We are driving out to the airfield in New Jersey to meet her plane. On the way we bought balloons and flowers.

My heart was beating so hard.

My heart will be beating so hard.

My heart is beating so hard.

Eliza comes with us. We both sit in the back and my dad complains he feels like a limo driver. But he smiles the whole way like he can hardly contain himself. After the e-mail a week ago, we got the actual phone call just two days ago with the schedule for arrival, the time and the place. My whole language arts and social studies class made cards that I had in my backpack, even though my dad tells me we should wait until she settles in to show her.

Ms. Jaffe had a special meeting with just me and we talked about all my fears. For some reason, knowing Eliza was waiting for me outside the door, I just let everything out. I talked and talked and talked.

"It's normal to feel that way," Ms. Jaffe explained. "A lot has happened in the past year. You've changed a lot and grown. And there will be some time for adjustment."

We had graduated to the guidance counselor's office so there were not alphabet posters for me to stare at. I was sitting in a big leather chair.

"Above all else," Ms. Jaffe said, "keep talking. Don't censor yourself or beat yourself up. If you feel like crying, cry."

Her permission made me feel better.

There are hundreds, or what feels like hundreds, of people at the landing strip. Mothers with babies in their arms and kids with signs. WELCOME HOME. WE MISS YOU. BEST MOTHER IN THE WORLD. BEST FATHER. NEW DADDY. PROUD TO BE AMERICAN.

Like walking, living bumper stickers. The love is nearly visible. The excitement is contagious.

"I should have made a sign," I say to Eliza.

"We just have to shout louder than anyone," she answers.

The plane is huge as it taxies closer and closer. I can hardly breathe. But maybe that's because I squeezed into last year's jeans and T-shirt. I wanted to wear something familiar. Something my mother would recognize.

When the plane wheels finally stop moving and the loud sound of the engine is cut, the door begins to open. The metal stairs are pushed into place. Suddenly the roar is deafening and I realize it is all the families. There is crying and shouting and even screaming. There is a baby wailing from having been woken up. I don't even know I am crying until my throat starts to hurt and I taste mucus on my lips.

Because I see her right away. She stands a minute at the top of the stairs like she is scared too. Like she is wondering if we will know who she is. Maybe for a split second she wonders if we are really here.

She is a little thinner than I remember, but she'll like that. Her face is tan. Her camouflage hat is in her hand. I watch as she pulls her hair out of her ponytail and gives her head a little shake.

"Mommy!" And my voice carries above the music of the families. She jerks her head toward us and the huge smile that spreads across her face tells me everything.

My mother is home safe.

forty-two

I t's not over completely. There are still moments when the magic is working. And there are moments when it doesn't, no matter how hard I want it to. And there are still moments when I get really mad for no reason, and I don't know why.

But today, Eliza and I are making paper dolls of Lester and Lynette so no matter what happens, we won't forget who they were. Like sometimes, I feel like I am forgetting who I used to be. I sure don't know who I am going to be. It's like being stuck in the Lemon Squeeze. It doesn't feel real good.

My mom is making us a snack before she has to leave for work. She got a new job at a pediatrician's office in town, but she makes sure to be home when I get back from school. The only thing I've noticed is that she gets up in the middle of the night sometimes. I hear her in the kitchen or when she turns on the television. Or once I saw her just sitting in the dark.

The quiet, she told me. She forgot the quiet.

"Lester doesn't look like that," Eliza tells me, inspecting my handiwork.

"How do you know what Lester looks like?"

Eliza smiles. "I know exactly what Lester looks like, don't you?"

We are sitting on my bedroom floor. I've always liked coloring. My mom drew the outline of the figures and we are filling them in with colored pencil. It's kind of babyish but it's relaxing.

"This is what he looks like," I say, but I don't really know anymore. Lester and Lynette feel like people I knew a long time ago. I remember them, but I can't really conjure up their faces. My Lester has brown hair and brown eyes. He looks kind of like Peter if I think about it, and I mention this to Eliza.

"You are boy crazy," she tells me. "I saw you talking to him in the hallway today."

"Who?"

"You know who," Eliza says. She is coloring in Lynette's long dress with the entirely wrong color.

"I don't *like* like Peter," I say, but she's right, sometimes I can't think of anything else but boys. Eliza and I made a new vow, a pact, in real life, and I am sticking to it. I could have as many boyfriends as I liked as long as I always remember who my best friend is.

I can do that.

"Well, I hope you'll be able to spell his name right, at least," Eliza says. Then she immediately throws her hand over her mouth.

"Okay, what are you talking about?"

"Nothing."

"Come on, tell me, Liza. You have to tell me now."

She is peeking out from her hand. Her eyes wide. "You won't get mad at me? You can't remember?"

"Swear I won't get mad." But of course, I can't really say that for sure. I can only remember that Eliza is my best friend and I need my best friend. Boys will come and go, just like Mrs. Smith said.

"Tell me already!"

"Well—" Eliza clearly doesn't want me to know something. She did something she shouldn't have and she's worried I'm going get upset. I know her so well. I want to put my arms around her and tell her there's nothing she could have done that would make me not like her anymore.

Love her.

So I do. And she tells me.

"I read your diary," she says. "The one you hid in the cabinet under the sink in the bathroom back at my house. The one where you wrote Michael's name over and over."

I am less upset than I'd thought I'd be. "So?" I say. "And?"

"You spelled his name wrong. Every time. Over and over. It's Michael, *M-I-C-H-A-E-L*. Not *E-A*." And then she waits.

I think about this for a minute. *Michael.* All the dreams I've made up come back to me, all the nights I spent fantasizing about ways I might run into him up at the hotel one day, and then like a movie-reel projector, the whole thing comes grinding to a halt. I can even hear the background music slowing down and getting all distorted.

"I did?"

She nods.

"I spelled his name wrong?"

She nods again.

"I spelled his name wrong, like, a hundred and fifty times?" A huge laugh is breaking out inside my stomach.

"Yeah, like, a hundred and sixty times. In pink magic marker!"

We are both squealing. There're lots of different kinds of magic.

"Imagination is more important than knowledge. For knowledge is limited to all we now know and understand, while imagination embraces the entire world, and all there ever will be to know and understand."

—*Albert Einstein*

winter 2005

There is still a war going on. It's on the news every day. Eight hundred and forty-one United States military have died in Iraq—this year alone.

And my mother is not one of them.

But hardly a day goes by I don't think, *She could have been.* Or that somebody else's mother or father is. It took me a long time after my mom got back, to not wake up in the middle of the night and worry if she was home or not. I can't even admit how many nights I crawled into my parents' bed.

"Peter's dad is going back," I say to my mom. "He wants to go back."

We are baking in the kitchen, like it's the most ordinary thing in the world, but it isn't. Not for me. My mom is here.

"I heard that too," my mom says.

"But why would he do that?"

We are making cupcakes for my class because tomorrow is my birthday. I'm going to be thirteen. My mother puts down the bowl and wipes her floury hands on her pants, just like she tells me not to do but these days she probably wouldn't say anything. Little things like that don't bother her anymore. If there has been any change, my mother is calmer since she's come home.

"I don't know, sweetie, and I imagine it's hard for Peter and his mother, but we should all be grateful there are soldiers like that."

"I am."

I am pulling apart the little paper liners and placing them one by one into the baking pan while my mom is stirring, a blue one, a red one, a yellow one. "Mom?"

"Yeah?"

"Mom?"

This time she just waits for me to talk. "Do you think it's silly that Eliza and I still play make-believe?"

"No, not at all," my mom says. "Sometimes when I was sitting for hours, waiting for incoming wounded, I thought I was going to go crazy, just waiting. Feeling scared—not knowing what was going to happen. Or what I was going to see."

"You were scared?"

"Sure, sometimes. So I would just play a game in my head, like pretending I was somewhere else. Doing something else."

We are ready to pour the batter into the little paper cups. "Hold the pan still," my mom tells me and she lifts the big bowl.

"Like what?" I ask.

"Well, I used to imagine I was at a dance, like a high school dance, with Daddy like when we were young. I used to think about what shoes I would be wearing, what color my dress was. What my hair looked like—you know."

"Did it help?"

"Definitely, I know it did." My mom fills each cupcake cup to the top and then puts down the bowl.

"Mom?"

"Yeah?"

"Can I ask you another question?"

"Surely." My mom opens the oven, slides the two cupcake pans inside, and shuts it with her foot.

"When you were my age, were you boy crazy?"

"No, I don't think so," she answered. "I was a bit slow in that department. I think I was still only interested in my Cabbage Patch dolls in seventh grade."

"Your what?"

She is smiling. "Wanna see them?"

"Really?"

"Sure, in the attic. C'mon."

So while my cupcakes are baking, we climb up the pull-down stairs and my mother shows me her Cabbage Patch doll collection, all their clothes, little boots, thermal blankets, hair clips—because, boy, do these dolls have hair—pink pacifiers, even make-believe diapers. My mom could remember not only the name each doll came with, but also the name she chose when she sent back the "adoption papers."

This afternoon, my last afternoon as a twelve-year-old, my mom and I sit cross-legged on the attic floor and we play. We are making up stories for what each doll has been doing all these many, many years, as my mother says. One of them, Gillian, just got married to her college sweetheart. Don is now a retired fireman who likes to take his boat out fishing. The one with the purple boots is a Vegas showgirl named Allison who just signed a modeling contract with Wilhelmina. The one with the dark hair is Tyler. He is a sports announcer now.

And nobody is happier today than I am, sitting up here with Mom, except maybe Gillian, and Don, and Allison, and Tyler.

Reading Group Guide for

The Summer Before Boys

Julia is the narrator. Think about how Eliza might tell the story.

Why does the author include a description of Eliza and Julia's identical nightgowns? *I could barely make out the faded kittens and puppies in the fabric. Little pink kittens and little blue puppies. . . .* (p. 6)

Why is time so important in the novel?

Mohawk Mountain Lodge was built in 1862. Why is the setting of this novel so important? Write an advertisement for the Mohawk Mountain Lodge. Include details of its setting and history.

What do you think Julia means when she thinks, *This is going to be a safe day?* (p. 11).

How does Julia's mom have bad timing as described in chapter three? What does bad timing mean? What other characters have bad timing in the novel?

What is the National Guard? Why does Julia's mom join the National Guard? When did she join? How old was Julia then? How does Julia react when her mother joins? What is good about the fact that her Mom is in the Guard?

When Julia's mom is about to ship out to Iraq, why does Julia fervently hope that she won't put on her hat?

What are some of the ways, the past, "the olden days" at the hotel were different from what Julia and Eliza experience in the current day? Think specifics—Travel? Clothing? Manners? Speech? Food?

Why does Pam say to Julia that she must be so proud of her mother? How does Julia react? How does Eliza comfort her?

What does Eliza mean when she says, "Nothing is different in the world."? (p. 26). Why does Julia disagree with her?

Do you think Mrs. Jaffe is helpful as a support system for Julia and Peter at school? Why does she make them uncomfortable?

In the "summers" before the current one how does Julia view her physical self?

What are some of the things that Julia knows about her mother's life as a nurse in Iraq?

In chapter six, Julia describes how her family starts fighting with each other right before her mom leaves for active duty? Why does this happen?

What are some of the ways Julia's imagination helps her cope? Later in the novel, does her mother talk about having a similar experience?

Photographs are important throughout the novel. Think about some of the times Julia looks at and thinks about photographs. Why does she have such an interest in them?

What does "magic" mean to Julia and Eliza? How does the concept of magic change in the novel?

In what ways is the flashback in chapter nine important to Julia's awareness of herself? How does the author create suspense in this scene? Why does Julia think, *I didn't feel like myself anymore*?

How does Eliza interact with Michael? Are her feelings and actions different from Julia's?

When Mrs. Jaffe asks Peter and Julia to write about their parents and the war and what it felt like to worry if your mom or dad is going to live or die—how does Julia react? How does Peter interact with Mrs. Jaffe? With Julia?

Why does Julia develop a sudden interest in horses? (p. 58)

Why does Eliza keep playing the past game?

In chapter twelve, when Julia sees the men in uniform how does she react? What are some of the ways that the author makes this scene very suspenseful?

Why does Julia recount stories of other women who have been killed in conflicts?

Why does Julia say "Shrek" when she knows Eliza is mad at her? Can having long-term connections, knowing the past and what kinds of things have happened to someone, help two people get over disagreements? How? (p. 80)

Why does Eliza always get the blame for everything that happens? (p. 101)

How does Michael figure out where Eliza might be? Why does Michael want everyone to think he is a hero?

Why does Peter tell Julia that he hates her? (p. 165)

What does the summer before boys mean? Julia calls it a slow process. What does she mean when she says about D'Ville . . . "I can't see the details anymore"?

Why is it significant that Julia spelled Michael's name wrong? Why does Eliza finally tell her about the fact that she spelled his name wrong?

Does Peter like Julia?

Is Julia "boy crazy"?

How has Julia's mom changed since she came home from Iraq?

What is the significance of Julia's mom's Cabbage Patch dolls?

Why don't we ever learn Julia's mom's name?